I0638565

# Color Me Jazzmyne

## A Novel by:

*Marian L. Thomas*
Best-Selling Author

Published By L.B Publishing
Atlanta, GA
www.lbpublishingco.com

Library of Congress Control Number: 2009920867

ISBN 978-0-615-27067-8

Printed in the United States of America

First Edition

# Color Me Jazzmyne

Reached #1
on Amazon.com®

L. B Publishing
Atlanta, GA

To:

My husband

My mother

My mother-in-law

My friends & family

My spoiled but playful Dog


Thank you for your love & support!

# Acknowledgments

I would also like to thank the editor who looked into the pages and saw something more than a story. I can't give thanks to anyone, however, without mentioning my interior book designer, who showed me that commitment to a project is still alive and well even in the world we live in today. Thank you very much!

There are many who offered their advice, put up with my rambling all the time and really gave me a listening ear. Thank you.

I know that I've thanked my husband, but I have to just say that I couldn't have gotten the courage to do something like this, if he wasn't the type of man that he is! Encouraging, caring and always ready to say, "you can do whatever you put your mind too." I now believe him.

# Contents

○ ◉ ○

# The Encounter

My name is Naya Moná. Some say, that I live what they would call a "once upon a time" dream. How I wish that were true. You see, every turn I made and every moment that flew by in my life, created a new color in my box, my crayon box that is. I made the choice to keep that box closed, until now.

There are moments in our lives when we are forced to open our boxes and expose our colors. For me, that moment had arrived. I woke up one morning with the sun glaring into the corners of my eyes, and the light from it, burning a sense of reality into my head. It was at this precise moment, that I realized, it was time to open my box, pick up the phone, and make a call to a son whom I hadn't seen since birth. I knew it would be difficult, hard, and very emotional for the both of us; and yet, this was a moment that neither could run from. It was a moment that we both would have to face. That was the beauty of reality, the nature of a moment.

Soon, he would ring my doorbell, enter into my home, and pull back the cover of my box— exposing my colors. He would force me to answer the question…What color is Jazzmyne?

Hear my story, listen to my voice, feel my emotions, follow my journey. Come into my box of colors, to discover the woman I've become. Listen, as I explain the moments that colored me Jazzmyne.

# PART ONE

# Chapter 1

"My past however, is something quite different. It still haunts me, slaps me in the face and dares me to face the reality of today. Every day, it seems, I am forced to remember what color is Jazzmyne."

## ○ ⊙ ○

# What Color is Jazzmyne

J ust the other day, I saw a little girl who reminded me of what peace looks like. Even now as I sit in this room waiting for him, I can still see a picture of her. It's so clear that I find myself reaching out to touch an image inside my head. She stood, just on the bank of the ocean, as if she were holding only the tip of her bare toes in the coolness of the water. She had her eyes closed, allowing the crisp waves of the water to sink deep into her veins, and run up to the pit of her stomach. This seemed to make her laugh, because a small smile slid across her face and her head tilted softly into a relaxed position. She looked so peaceful and sure of herself as she stood just watching her reflection dance upon the water, playing off the sunlight and smiling at the clouds.

Life was once like that for me—peaceful and serene, with not a care to steal the sunshine away. That is how it should be for a child.

My past however, is something quite different. It still haunts me, slaps me in the face and dares me to face the reality of today. Every day, it seems, I am forced to remember what color is Jazzmyne. Once upon a time the color of snow ran through me. It ran so deep that it blended with my insides, messed with my emotions and played with the deepest corners of my heart.

How can life do that to a woman? As I look into the mirror, I can quickly see the colors that answer that question.

Upon the walls of my office are newspapers encased in gold frames. I glance at the writings, the ink still trying to hold on to the paper. So many years have passed. They all told a story. Each one represented a version of some reporter's dream. Some wrote that I became everything from simply nothing. Others wrote that my voice awakens them, and breathes life into the deepest corner of their being. I wish it did the same for me. I could use an awakening. I stop and pause in front of my window. How I can still see that little girl, the picture of course is not as faded as it ought to be, the light has left, the clouds have come raging in and the sun, well, it appeared to have left some time ago.

I was still gazing out the window, struggling to get that picture out my head when I heard the knock upon my door. I could feel my nerves as they came crashing upon me. My story, my life, is about to unfold.

Once again, I will become a color in a crayon box. I will tell him how the colors began to mix in my life.

He stands before me as I sit upon a soft white leather chair. I can see him taking it all in. I say nothing. I try to imagine his expression as he pulled up to my home, I could see his eyes gazing over the acres of lush landscaping, settling for a moment, on one of the gardens that surround the property, admiring the beauty of the waterfall within it.

Maybe that doesn't do it for him. Maybe, just maybe, it's the way the driveway seems to never end, or perhaps it's the way the house sits up on the mountain, commanding the attention of the flowers below. I've heard it said that one can smell the richness of this house a mile away.

Now here he is, standing in my office, soaking it all up, trying to imagine how it would have been to grow up in the midst of all of this. I knew that as he walked in, he'd seen the first-edition prints on the walls and felt his feet sink into the smoothness of the plush carpet. I knew that he had stood at the bottom of the stairs, just before placing a foot on the first step and glanced around at the other staircases that seemingly flowed from each corner of the house. I imagined his mind wondering what my life was all about.

In a moment, I'm about to break the silence that still exist between us. I'm about to take the mystery out of his thinking, correct his wild and highly mistaken conclusions. I'm going to tell him just what color is Jazzmyne. After all, he feels he has a right to know.

Time seems to stand between us, moving at a turtle's pace. I glance upon him and I see his eyes twitch upward. I listen, and I swear I can hear my heart begin to thump right through the silk threads of my blouse. I feel the movement of my mouth and then the words "my son" drapes off my lips.

I catch him staring at me, wondering if it could really be so, if I could really be his mother. There is no hello, no hug and of course, no small talk. We both are sitting now, ready to put it all on the table, saying to ourselves that we won't hold anything back. It sounds good only inside our minds. I find myself lost in the shadows of the past as I watch him. I glance into his light blue eyes and immediately I find myself being taken back in time, back to the years of tears. However, I know that it's not time to go back there yet so I still say nothing.

He's right next to me now, gazing into my twilight hazel-brown eyes. I watch his hand reach out and touch the creamy complexion of the skin on my left arm. I felt the tremble in his touch. There was something about the strength in his hands that told me so much and then left me knowing nothing at all, except here stood a man.

He is tall; taller than I expected. His shoulders are broad and his brown hair so curly that I can tell he hates it. He reaches up and without realizing it runs his fingers through it, almost in disgust. How I remembered looking at him when they put him in my arms, he was so small and swaddled. I was thinking that he was just as white as white could be. Nothing it seemed had changed about that fact.

Actually, as I sat there taking him all in, I saw there wasn't a trace of me in him from his hands to his feet. It's ironic how the color of snow appears to have seeped deeply into the veins of my son.

Yet, as I close my eyes even for a brief moment, ignoring his impatience with this—I can still remember holding his tiny little hand in mine and wondering what his life would become. I had been a quarters throw from thirteen then.

I let out a long sigh as I open my eyes. He's so close to me that I can smell his anger. I can feel his suspicion and his haunting thoughts that he was not wanted or that I just didn't care. How I want to tell him that it wasn't like that. In fact, I want to scream it from the top of my lungs and allow it to flow out from the tips of my toes.

I admit that I long to hear him call me Mother, Mama or anything that would lift my spirits and remove emotions that are present inside me. But I know it's too soon for such a request.

I need courage, strength, to tell him, to have my life unfold right in front of him. Someone once told me that strength comes from within, so I dig deep. I feel like I'm looking into a bottomless well that has long dried up— not a drop of strength in sight.

I knew he was waiting. He can't even say my name and yet he's still here, still waiting and watching. Shall I begin with a *"once upon a time"* type of story, or would he see through that fairytale? I sigh again. I know that this upsets him because I can see him trying to hold back the fact that he wants to hit me on the back and make the words flow off my tongue that he has come to hear. Patience is a virtue, of course, who knew it would be put to the test between a once-upon-a-time mother and a once-upon-a time son.

Finally, I open my mouth but then I catch him staring at something. His eyes are focused upon my dresser.

He's looking at a small picture that sits just on the corner of my fireplace mantle. He's staring at a picture of me holding him. I try to hold back my emotions but my mind quickly begins to drift off to the day when I held him so tight before I had to say good night.

That was the day that I planted my first mother's kiss upon his baby smooth cheek and told him to never forget me, to think about me in his sweet little dreams. Foolishness now, it seems. I had even whispered into his right ear as if he could actually understand me then, "Mommy loves you little one."

How quickly I am snapped back into reality, as the tears begin to flow to the tip of my cheeks and then linger there, just on the end, hovering on the brink of my words.

I see him look at me as they began to run furiously from the corners of my eyes, hitting the top of my shirt, as if a faucet had been turned on. I know that he's looking at me and thinking that it's all a performance, something to feign a sign of emotion.

He gets up ready to head toward the door, I reach for him. The tips of my fingers glaze upon his skin and I thought I saw a flicker of hope, a spot of love, a speck of forgiveness. It was just a thought.

He's almost at the door now, but something inside him tells him to stop. He turns quickly back toward me while shooting me a look that sends me into a frenzy. The faucet is still turned on and the tears are gushing out, darn near slobbering all over myself. I watch as he walks back over and you can see the tiny wrinkles in his face just around his eyes. He sits, but I can smell the anger that's in the air.

He's so determined to hear this; after all, this is why he's here. I muster up some courage from a well near mine and wipe away the tears. I take one deep breath and then another one; this is not going to be easy, as life never is.

I can feel my mouth opening and the words slowly finding their way to my lips. *Okay,* I say to myself. I try to picture myself on stage for the very first time. *I got through that*—I can get through this, is all I can mutter inside my head. He still hasn't said a word, but I know his heart is listening.

○ ◉ ○

# Chapter 2

"I could go into the vivid details but the pain still takes hold of me and grips onto my very being not ever letting go it seems. What can I say but, 'Once upon a time.'"

○ ◉ ○

# Once Upon a Time

When I was twelve years old I sat down and took hold of a pencil, slid the tip of it into a sharpener making sure it was sharpened just right. When that was accomplished to my satisfaction, I pulled it out ensuring that it stayed firmly between my fingers. I then watched as I made it glide upon a blank piece of paper creating my future.

*I can hear the rain fall on my window. I close my eyes and I can feel each drop, misty yet refined, cool and refreshing like sweet candy canes. The peace seems to overwhelm me, but I can still hear the rain upon my*

*window. Caught up on a raindrop, I want it to carry
me away, want it to float me back up into that cloud
in the sky, never to fall back down to the pain that
awaits me on earth. I wipe away the tears, but I can
still hear the rain fall upon my window. Shall I try to
catch them—the rain drops or the tear drops? To me,
they feel the same. Can you hear the raindrops, the
raindrops on my window?*

Just before I wrote that song, my father had just finished punishing me by restricting me from playing my
Atari. I remember how I cried my eyes out that night as I
watched the rain pour outside my window. It was the
emotions inside of me that the rain helped soothe away,
that caused me to write those lyrics. They were simple, yes,
but true. The rain felt cool and refreshing just like the tears
that had run down my cheek.

That night I cried over an Atari game. But many nights
and then years later, life, he, me, handed me so much more
to scream about. He'd been a father to me then, but just as
quickly as my tears had stopped and the rain had dried, so
he stopped. I could go into the vivid details, but the pain

still takes hold of me, grips onto my very being, not ever letting go.

So how else can I start this story except with "Once upon a time...?" I won't tell you that up until I was thirteen, I led a fairy tale of a life. Far from it. My father and I weren't poor just living one day and dying the next. Mother had passed away while giving birth to me. They say she screamed to take me away from him, but at that time, everyone thought her pleas were mere side effects induced from the labor pains. If only they'd known what type of man stood before them.

I laugh now when I try to picture that scene, and then I cry because she knew what was inside him. She was the only one that saw past the smile on the outside. She knew the man I once called Father, Daddy and Provider. She knew what he would do to me, because he had in fact, done the same to her. My mother, if she lived, would have been my sister.

Years later, it's still beyond weird to think about. Sick and downright unthinkable, but it's true. She had been his daughter. Enough said.

We lived, Father and I on the West side of Chicago in a small but somewhat comfortable apartment building called the Vista View, only there wasn't a view unless you counted the alleyway when you pulled back the shade of my bedroom window. I think there had at one time been something in the back you could call a vista, but barely a trace remained by the time I lived there.

I'm not telling you all this so that you can roll out the red carpet or pull out the Kleenex. I'm telling you this to prove to you that, for me, there really was a "once upon a time."

My father, Jonathan Kenneth Creek, was a white man with blue eyes and wavy brown hair. He stood over six feet with shoulders that seemed always to be leaning more toward the ground than anything else. He was slender, too thin some said, but he was cocky and had an air of confidence about him. Up until I turned thirteen, he was the greatest man I knew.

Sure he drank too much, partied too hard, but he never missed a school play, was home to greet me when I walked in the door, and always loved to listen to me sing. He would sit for hours as I practiced singing for this or that and wouldn't say a word; just listened.

He would make me feel special when he did that and often helped me to forget his not-so-kind qualities.

For a child, a parent always being there is like cotton candy that never seems to run out. Some thought he was a hero raising his daughter on his own. I did too, once upon a time.

But that was it. My twisted version of a fairytale life came and went with a thunder so loud, that the memory of it all still makes me want to slap somebody. I was thirteen then, and for me I thought my life had just begun to shoot up like a rocket on a cloudless summer day. I imagined from there it would be like the movies, all stars and bright lights. I remember that day like I'm still there; and in some ways I was.

It was the day I had finally managed to land the lead role in the school play. It had been my first. It's not that I wanted to become an actor, but the part involved lots and lots of singing since it was a musical, a love story. I remember waking up that day to find a big box upon my bed.

One can only imagine the joy I felt to find inside the box a book—a very large one on learning to write songs. I had wanted that book for years but we never could afford it. I remember holding it so close and promising to read it every day. Dreams do come true I thought. Life was like sunshine, nice and warm and I felt like butter underneath it.

That night, my Father came into my room just before we left for the play. I remember looking at him, all dressed up in his only suit and thinking he was the most handsome daddy I knew. It was like peaches and cream, with just a hint of chocolate to sweeten the picture.

"You look beautiful," he said.

Little did I know that it would be the last kind word I'd get from him, the last time I'd ever call him Daddy. Even now, it still makes me want to cry. My heart still wants to break, but it has already been broken a dozen times, and frankly, I am tired of trying to put the pieces back together again.

He'd been the one to break it the first time, to shattered a child's heart. With one touch, he took it all away. I have wished so many times that I could ask him why and how could he do such a monstrous thing to his own daughter. But what good would it really do? It certainly wouldn't have set me free.

Anyway, that night, they say I sang my heart out. That night, they said the world heard and listened to the voice of a child. I remembered the emotions that seemed to explode inside me as I'd stepped onto that stage and uttered my very first note. I had sung, I think, for the mother I'd had never known. The sister I'd never had.

I imagined what it would have been like to have her sitting out in that audience, and in my heart, I'd sung to the empty chair that should have held her. It was a feeling I had never had or expressed before. A memory that I thought I would never find.

I pause for a moment, I felt the need to stop and turn to my son, and I just wanted to ask....had to know.

"Has that ever happened to you? Perhaps not, perhaps you have no memories or just pretend not to, just to be you, to be here in this moment." I looked at him as I said this and saw no emotion, not even a stinking twitch. He was too much like me. *Here I go again*, getting back on track but I couldn't help but say out loud....

"You know, already, there is a memory being formed in you." I continued not sure if he was listening, not caring. "Perhaps your memory is not as deep as mine, but I know that it's there—you know, in the core of the heart, in the part that never goes away completely no matter how hard you try to walk away from it or forget it's there, it's the part that seems to cry all the time. Perhaps you feel that this memory is just in my mind. Perhaps, you're right. Always remember not to push it too deep; don't let it go so far back that when you reach for it, it just hurts."

Now where was I...? Oh yes.

Standing on that stage had been like watching your favorite love story. It captured me and took me places I never dreamed of. I had found myself in love—in love with music, with the stage, with the thrill of moving people to stop and just listen.

What a feeling to move someone with your lyrics, to push the thoughts of their mind so that they focus on the command of your throat, the length of your voice and respond. It had been as if my voice were saying to everyone….Close your eyes…listen.

*Can you hear the music playing inside my head? Can you here the song that explodes upon my lips? Can you hear the notes that urge me to try and try to reach their potential, their height, breadth and depth?*

Each note became more than just something burning inside me. They tore me wide open, ripped into my core and planted even more lyrics into my very being. I'd felt like I was ready to grow and spout with a voice that shook and awakened every part of who I was or could be.

The music was like ice-cold Kool-Aid sliding down my throat on a hot summer day. I embraced it and in turn, the music stretched out and wrapped its arms around me and promised to never let go. With every stroke of a note I felt like I was holding on tight. In fact, I'd felt like I had been doing more than singing, I was embracing the beautifulness of sound.

How often I would love to go back to that very moment and feel once again the music wash over me like tides of water. I would love to be able to look into that audience again and see a man smiling with so much pride that it made me sing even harder. No one knows what it felt like to lose him, to lose my childhood, my fairytale, to have it all gone in one disgusting touch.

That night is where it all began for me. It was the night I developed my dreams, the night I discovered who I wanted to be. It was a night that shattered everything inside of me and left me turned inside out. It was a night that brought me to right here, right now, at this very moment. That night started it all, ended it all, and made me who I am today: Jazzmyne, the jazz singer.

○ ◉ ○

# Chapter 3

"The color of Jazzmyne, I realized then, was a mixture not only of the memories of the past but of the realities of it— and then there were what I call the secret hues. These lay concealed beneath even what was on the surface, these were hues of something more, colors that were seemingly deeper, unreachable even."

# The Color of
# Jazzmyne Runs Deep

The play was over, the ride home had begun. I remember him having this silly smile on his face, grinning as if he had already started to turn his mind over to something sad. We stopped for ice cream, something we never had money for. It was "my night" he said. You should have seen the way he carried on, telling everyone how his little woman sang her heart out. I never knew; never saw what was coming next. Never saw the hues behind the smile.

I could tell you what happened that night, right down to the very stank of his cologne but I won't. I won't allow myself to go through that nightmare again, not even for you. But I can tell you that when it was over, when it was said and done, my childhood went with it. I will tell you this because I think it's important to know, that I fought, I screamed and I cried.

However, for me, there was no one to hear that sad song. No audience, no one to give me a hand.

It was just me, just me. It was like someone was slapping me over and over again, and no matter how hard I tried to stop it, the pain just kept coming, until the lights went out and the tears stopped, and I was left with just a shell of me.

You ask if he was drunk. No. Was he crazy? Maybe? Did it matter? Drunk, crazy or just plain insane, it was still all the same. It was everything.

You might wonder why I didn't call the police, why I didn't tell someone. I can't answer that. I can't tell you why when I went to school the next day, I didn't tell my teachers. I can't tell you why I didn't run away. Truth of the matter was I was more than afraid. My heart was terrified.

You see, when you're thirteen and something like this happens you ask yourself many questions. In fact, you began to feel like maybe you did something to deserve it. Basically, you lie to yourself in order to deal with it. You deny it happened even when it continues to happen. I don't know why I reacted that way. I had felt like I was trapped in a corner with my arms crossed and my eyes closed. But I could see the front door. It was as if the door had been staring at me even through the confines of my fingers, and yet not one inch of my body would move.

There were moments when I would pack and head to the door but then reality threw me a quick slap and I remembered I was just a kid. Where would I go? Better yet, who would believe me? Every day was a nightmare.

And then, one day the nightmare became something more; I was pregnant. Bam! There it was a taste of reality that had been growing in my stomach.

In fact, when I had finally come out of the haze that I appeared to have drifted in and took note of what was happening to me, I had been five months into it. He'd known all along. How could he have not? Every morning I was sick, and he would sit back and watch. My clothes began to fit tighter and tighter, so he found the money to buy me bigger ones.

He would sit back in that chair of his, at that same rotten kitchen table and just watch as my stomach began to grow and everything I ate found its way out of me. Often, I wanted to just reach out and slap that sickening smile off his face. I hated to look at him. I hated to breathe, to live, to cry. And even to sing.

I was caught in the middle of my own sad song, not like country music or even like blues; but it was more like jazz without words, sometimes smooth, sometimes dissonant and overbearing.

The day had come for me to give birth; another life was born.  The pains hit me so hard I thought I would die. Honestly, I wanted to.  No one knows how it feels to have your father's child inside of you and to feel guilty for loving that child. How do you explain it?

When he was born, on my way to the hospital, the wind was light and I remember looking up into the sky and taking note of how beautiful it was.  It was calming in some strange way. He, Father that is, had been there, of course, watching and waiting. I didn't realize that he was waiting for a girl to come out of me. I didn't know. How could I?

When I heard the first cry I cried right along. In fact, as the drugs had begun to take their toll on my body, I swore it was as if I had heard the cry of another child. It was the drugs I was sure.

I still remember how I wanted to hold him in my arms forever and never let him touch my child. The nurse, I remember, had been so impressed by how beautiful he was. His skin was so soft, so smooth I could have rubbed it all night.

Even now I still recall how furious he was. To see the look upon his face when she announced that it was a boy brought a smile to my face. I didn't understand why then, but it just did. He had stormed out of the door, cussing and screaming and demanding to know how.

The nurse had thought he was just upset because his daughter had gotten pregnant so young. Reality is often there staring us in the face, and yet we choose to ignore it, even when we need to see it the most.

She had been the one to take the picture I saw my son staring at. It became the only thing I had to remember him by—that and my dreams.

I needed to take a breather now so that I could catch my thoughts. I needed to direct my son away from the past and bring him into the present. I didn't look at him, didn't need to. His eyes were staring into the patterns of my voice, watching their every movement. All I had to do was flex my throat in his direction.

"You see, you judge the outside while I know the inside. You were taken from me in the middle of the night as I slept. The hospital had given me something to help me sleep and I didn't even know you were gone until the next day when I awoke and you were no longer in my arms. That was the beginning of my "once upon a time." I had given birth to a son whom I'd never even gotten a chance to name."

"Even now, you stare at me as if I could have done something or should have said something. But think about it, you were once there yourself; how much control did you have at thirteen? You think I had it easier than you, that I should have made decisions, taken matters in my own hands, don't you? You're right, I should have decided to open my mouth and tell them that I was his daughter and that you were his son, but would that have helped?"

"They would have taken you away and still this moment would be upon us and you would still be sitting here, listening to me as I start a story that begins with 'once upon a time' and ends with me, for a brief moment having looked into the eyes of my father's son."

I could see, even now, the shock of it all upon his face, so I turned to him and said in a manner that only a mother whose life has thrown her a couple of quick hooks to the left could, "Take a moment, please, to let it all sink in. In fact, take as much time as you need. Don't worry, I've had fifty-plus years."

Then I got up, walked over to the door, turning my head, watching as he placed his face into his hands.

Knowing that my heart wanted to run over to him and embrace him like a real mother, but who was I fooling? Real was just a version of my life.

Outside the room, I instantly fell upon the wall, allowing the first tear to fall. Not wanting to hold them back, not trying to control them. The tears burst through like the sun after a storm; you might say that the tears took on the colors in my box. They began to represent the different moods that I was in. If they were light and barely touching the skin it seemed, then they were colors of laughter and happiness. If they were tears like today, then they were colors of storms filled with lightening and loud thunder.

I tried to get control of myself but the emotions—the pain, the sorrow had begun to build in me the strong desire to tell him to just leave. Isn't that weird? Why lie about it, I hated telling him all of this, hated having him see me in such disarray. I hated hearing myself say the words that I knew must come out of my mouth. Most of all, I hated seeing the look upon his face.

Hated facing the blame and finally the questions I knew was coming at the end. It all made me want to respond by saying, "Why do you want to know what can't be changed?"

It certainly can't put him back in my arms again. I can't go back and hold him close to my heart and listen as his heartbeat synched with mine. I certainly can't go back and try to rub his smooth baby skin and allow myself to get lost in his sweet, innocent softness. The reality of it all is that those moments will never happen for us—not today and not tomorrow; perhaps, not ever. So what was the point?

I knew that I needed to go back in that room and face him but it; the story, that is, was pulling me apart. *Close your eyes and try*, I keep whispering inside my head. It wasn't working.

Now I feel like screaming but I knew he deserved the truth. Doesn't everyone? I found myself standing in front of my office door, thinking. Telling myself to muster up that boldness, to reach deep for that courage and grab hold of it as if my life depended upon it. In many ways, that was not far from the truth.

Finally, I feel my nerves responding. Slow, but the tingling that tells me to move, is starting to take place. I place my hand upon the door knob and begin to turn it, all the while knowing that he would still be sitting there, waiting for more. What else was there to tell? What else really mattered?

He was there, but not as I pictured. He was standing, leaning up against the wall holding that picture in his hands. When my eyes caught sight of the tears that were streaming down his face, I cried even more. Forget the storm of tears; I think I saw the colors of a tornado on the horizon in my heart.

There I just stood, crying like a child who had lost the most precious thing in her life, neither of us saying a word. Once again, the urge to wrap my arms around him and comfort him, came over me with a sudden swiftness, but I found my body telling me to refrain. There was something in his eyes that told me to keep my distance. Was that a mother's instinct? Probably not.

In the room, you could hear the crickets as they say. The silence between us was louder than our own body movements.

I wondered how long we would live in this moment. Would my son's hatred for me, ever be replaced with love and compassion? I was still fixated on that thought, when my heart jumped and my ears caught wind that we were moving into the next moment.

It was a shocking sound.

The sound was so loud. It was the type of sound that you hear when your heart can't take another beat. I saw it, but it was too late as the picture found its way to the floor and the glass began to shatter and my memories along with it.

"Why?" I screamed. He didn't answer me. Instead, he just stood there and looked at the broken glass that seemed to land ever so neatly upon the floor.

The picture had ripped almost in half, like this moment, it too was split between the past and the present. I reached to pick up it up, but when I did, he reached out and grabbed my hands. They were cold.

"Don't touch it. Just leave it on the floor."

I wanted to scream at him, but I already knew why he'd done it. His dreams, his life, even a part of his reality had been shattered. The destruction of the picture was just a reminder of how quickly it all went.

I didn't move, frozen, my hands still holding his. I could feel the blood rush through them. I wanted to cry upon his shoulders and tell him how sorry I was, but just as quickly as the glass had shattered, so did the moment. It was time to end the silence.

"Jonathan, I can't take back the past." I blurted out. "I can't even replace the present, and I certainly can't tell you about the future. But you came here to hear the truth, and I presented it to you very much like this picture—protected by glass. What is it that I can say that will undo what has been done? What is there that I can say that will cause the pain to go away? There is nothing."

"I want to hear it all, Jazzmyne." Finally, he spoke. "Or is Naya, your real name? I want to hear how you lived your life so tragically without me..... I want to hear what I came to hear, not what I already knew."

My heart stopped as the sting of his words sank deep into my brain cells. I looked up into his blue eyes and I saw fire, the flames of something I knew we could never come back from. It was something that, if we could ever move beyond this moment, would always have to remain trapped in the past. It would always remain a skeleton in my box. *Was there enough room in there?* I found myself pondering, and then as his words mulled around in my head, I began to ask myself...How could he know?

Terror struck me, as I sank to the floor. It was my turn to place my hands over my face, hoping to hide the thoughts that had been present upon it.

The color of Jazzmyne, I realized then, was a mixture not only of the memories of the past but of the realities of it—and then there were what I call the secret hues. These lay concealed beneath even what was on the surface, these were hues of something more, colors that were seemingly deeper, unreachable even.

I didn't know what to say, but I needed to know how much he knew. I wanted to ask…. "What color is Jazzmyne?" But instead, I sat back, folded my hands in my lap, not looking up at him. I couldn't. I knew that asking that question, now, at this moment, would reveal too much that he wasn't ready for. I thought the silence had knocked on the door again and let itself in but then, he surprised me. He opened his mouth. I think I stopped breathing for a second.

"Why do you try to play me, as if I can't tell that you're holding something back? You think I would come up here and not do my own research? If you don't start talking, then I will, and I'm sure the press will like my version of the story much better." There was nastiness in his tone, but I let him continue. He placed his hands in the air, mimicking a headline reading. "Ms. Jazzmyne, the famous jazz singer gave up her son to the world that she claimed to move with her gift of song. I can see the headlines, Jazzmyne—or should I call you mother to juice it up? You want me to be moved by your tears and your pain and even by what he did to you. I'm not. Did you think that I'd just say that it wasn't your fault or that it was beyond your control? I want the truth, not versions of it. Just the reality of it all!"

*Okay*, I thought, *here we go*....my crayon box was opening and a color was popping up.

"You want what you aren't ready to hear, I said. And neither am I ready to discuss it. Yes, to answer your question, it would be nice to hear you call me Mother; anything but my name. You will show me some respect or you will leave; with or without the reality of it all as you so poetically put it. That fact, is not complicated, but rather simple and easily carried out."

"It might not be Mother today, at this moment. But I swear to you, that never will you call me by my name— not now, not ever! In fact, listen to me carefully, so as not to miss one syllable.... If I even get the whiff of your trying to even mutter my name, off that quick to speak tongue, you will understand and feel what color I am!"

I saw the slight trace of a smile slide over his face and I wondered whether this heartless man could be my son. But then I remembered who I once was, and immediately, I knew without a doubt. Remember, I told you, the color of Jazzmyne runs deep.

I got up and, without looking at him, walked back over to the sofa and sat down. I focused my eyes on the dresser and I could almost see that picture still intact. *I ought to throw him out just for that*, I thought. *Close the box, girl...*"Okay," I said to myself.

It's funny how things change so quickly and yet remain the same. I still didn't look at him, although I know he's looking at me. I could feel the heat from his blaze, but at that moment, I didn't care—not one bit. Actually, I felt the need to return it, even hotter. Throw it right in his face. Was that the old Jazzmyne or the reformed Naya? Did it matter? I decided to answer the question for myself.

"Do you know how many colors are in a crayon box?" He didn't answer. "They say that in a crayon box one can make many colors just by mixing a couple together and then out comes a new box made up of new colors."

"You could say that some of the new colors still derive from the old ones and perhaps, in that case they are still the same. However on the other hand, you might say that one has nothing to do with the other. I guess it's how you look at the crayon box, isn't it?" I smiled directly at him. I could be like that sometimes.

○ ◉ ○

# Chapter 4

"Freedom in the darkness was for me, a piece of sweet
candy given to a child who had never tasted it.
It was that good and then some."

○ ◉ ○

# Freedom In the Darkness

How do you know what's in the darkness? And more, how do you know darkness really exists? Can you reach out and touch it? Freedom in the darkness was for me, a piece of sweet candy given to a child who had never tasted it. It was that good and then some. Every night, I would sit on my bed and just look out into the darkness, wondering what it could bring—if it would bring me something, not in a fearful way, as most children think, but something hopeful. I'd long to escape into it. I'd wonder whether, if I stared into it long enough, if I could blend into it, you know, just get lost in the darkness. After all, the daylight brought me no hope. Nothing real, that is.

Since having my son was not in the beast's plan for me—beast is what I now referred to him as, I became something horrible in his eyes. Many nights came were he would scream at me, accuse me of doing horrible things, lash out at me, only to then lock me in my room, forcing me to sit in the darkness void of the one thing I, a child, still needed the most, love from her parent. That is how the darkness, became my friend.

I would close my eyes and pretend that I was escaping into the darkness. Running into a place where the beast no longer existed in my life, to a place where I would never feel his touch crawl onto my skin, even to just say hello. You see, the darkness, became to me, a child's dream. It allowed me to dream of "happily ever after" stories; to see myself dancing in the moonlight, drifting on a butterfly that I imagined would light up the sky and carry me away.

I would ask the butterfly to please take me there, into the darkness, so that I could see what freedom means, but it would never respond, never answer a child's request. It was like a piece of the future that I could see but couldn't quite catch hold of. I keep reaching for it and yet it always seemed so far away.

In the beginning of my little games of imagination, I first thought the darkness was cruel, some sick joke meant to rip what little was still left of me. It would be there, staring me in the face, as if it were pleading with me to run into it, but when I would try, the door would slam shut and the bright lights of reality would come flooding in. I hated the word, reality, for a long time.

What did it really mean? For me, it was everything that I thought would never be. Freedom in the darkness.

For the next four years, reality kicked me in the face and then told me to turn the other cheek so that it could do it over and over again. Here I go again, another tear drop. Man!

The summer of my seventeenth birthday had come in with a sudden rush. The beast had finally decided to go out one night. It was the first time in four years that he had left me completely alone and didn't lock the door behind him.

Watching him walk out the door that evening was like watching someone hand me a million dollars. I could see it happening but, I still found that I wanted to pinch myself on the arm and ask, "Is this really happening?"

For three-and-half years, I'd been waiting for the moment to come when I could reach over and give myself a pinch. I'd put away every dime I could find. I did odd jobs whenever the beast allowed me to. When he was asleep, often I would check the couch for anything that jingled or was green.

Hidden underneath my bed, tucked in a corner, a bag of clothing were there, ready for the taking. The darkness had been screaming my name for months, and finally, I was ready to let its freedom become my reality. My heart beat out of my skin at the thought—the reality, that freedom was just a few steps outside the door. My sad song had turned into a sweet melody. I could taste it and feel it, and soon, I would be floating in it. This was my moment, perhaps even the beginning of my fairytale.

I had reached for the doorknob, bag in tow, when the first pains hit me. They hit me so hard that I fell to the floor and began to scream with all my might. No one, it seemed, heard me. Funny, kind of ironic perhaps, but the truth of the matter was that in my neighborhood, screams were quite common.

I want to take a moment and describe the pain for you, why? That is not a question so much as a response to something unknown. See, I wish to help you make the unknown, known, by making you live through my pain. Cruel, sick, and perhaps uncaring of me, you might say, but then those things are exactly what my pain was made of.

It was like a beating in my guts, like a ripping of my flesh. It was life, being taken away from me. That was the cruel and sick, reality of it all. I had lost life, precious life and I'd felt powerless to stop it. I couldn't control it or even fight against it happening.

The pain, the reality, both had been there. Every gut-wrenching moment was like something you pray you never feel again. There was that word again, reality. The reality side told me—it was a pain that I would feel again. Perhaps not at this degree, perhaps it would be something more, something worse. The pain side told me—it would always be there, waiting for me. Nevertheless, they were both, my enemies.

When I awoke, I was still on the floor. For a moment, I thought the pain had left, but you know reality never lets it be that easy. No, reality laughs at you, smacks you in the face, and then turns around and beats you over the head. The pain returned. I laid there with my eyes closed and cried.

After a while, the pain began to subside. The tears began to come to a halt and I felt as if I could finally move. I started with just a small tilt of my head. I noticed that my bag of clothes had disappeared. It was at this point, something else crept into my box and created a new color, it was filled with rage.

Evidently, the beast had come home, seen me there, and made the choice to ignore me. They say hatred is a word that should never be spoken, but I swear if I had a drop of strength left, at that moment, I would have screamed it from the roof tops!

Inside my head, the unthinkable thoughts were forming. I had a strong desire to kill him. Wrong or right, I couldn't deny those feelings existed. However, reality smiled at me for the first time. It told me to wake up and stop thinking stupid!

As I picked myself off that floor, reality threw me another grin. It reminded me that the door was still there, unlocked.

My body was weak and my legs had begun to shake as I tried to find the strength, a speck, to stand up straight. My mind was telling me to run—don't think, just open the door and run.

Once again, I reached for the knob. Pain, blood, tears, I didn't care. I knew then and there that I was leaving.

I was seventeen years old when I walked out into the world and my life became my own.

Okay, minor correction: I *thought* my life would become my own. I thought my fairytale was about to begin. Finally, I was going to go out into the world and I would...well, that it seemed, was the part I couldn't finish. You see, the moment I took off my jacket and wrapped it around my waist, reality stood in front of me and laughed its ugly head off!

I had only gotten a few blocks down the street, inching it seemed, away from the Vista View Apartments when I began to think that maybe I should turn around and go back. Crazy, I know. Unthinkable, you might say, but here was the situation from my viewpoint at the time. I was seventeen with no place to lay my head, no job in sight and the only clothes I owned were on my back.

But then I remembered that I had a thousand dollars in my pocket, and that became the very thought that made me smile back at reality and tell it to keep rolling! For a moment, or maybe for a split second, I felt like superwoman.

It was twelve o'clock when I finally made it to the subway and purchased my train ticket. It was funny, but it was only when the man placed my ticket in the confines of my hands and I gripped it with all my vital force, that the realization of freedom began to sink in.

I can't explain what that felt like but maybe this will help. Have you ever been so hungry, I mean downright starving when suddenly someone offers you a plate filled with steak and potatoes? Not just steak and potatoes but steak and potatoes that are topped with melted cheese and sliced mushrooms?

The aroma alone knocks you off your feet, but then you take your fork and your knife and cut just a tiny piece of the most seasoned, seared-to-perfection steak you've ever tasted, you place just that tiny piece in your mouth. As you begin to move your mouth, really getting into the grove of the chewing action, a sense of pure satisfaction fills you to your brim, and you just sit back and savor the moment. For me, seeing that ticket in my hands was better.

I rode the subway to the bus station. I walked up to the ticket booth, and when the woman asked me where I would like to go, I just broke out in tears. Now, I don't mean just a few drops sliding down my cheeks; I cried like there was no tomorrow. The woman tried to get me to calm down, but I just couldn't. The moment became too much for me, to think and do; even to communicate. It was much more complicated than just stopping tears. I was adding another color to my box.

The woman came out of her booth and asked me if I needed to sit down. I still had not found the ability to speak or stop the tears.

"Do you need me to call someone for you?" She asked.

"No," I finally said, as my eyes searched her face, watching her expression and wondering if I were making a big mistake talking to her.

"Are you hurt? Did someone hit you?" She asked.

"No," is all I could find the nerve to stumble out my mouth.

"Then why is there blood all over your jeans?"

I just sat there and tried hard to pull myself together, but the tears kept coming. How I wished they would stop, even if just for a moment. She pulled me up by the hand and told me to come with her.

Now terrified, my mind raced and my heart screamed. I keep thinking, "What if she turns me in? What if she made me go back?" She took me into an office and, when she closed the door behind her, I thought my fairytale of freedom was once again, locked outside.

"Now, you are going to have to tell me what happened, or else I will have to call the police." she said. I looked up at her and when my mouth finally opened, it all came spilling out and landing, it seemed, right in her lap. It just shot out of me uncontrollably until she turned me off.

When I was done, I'd felt like someone had slowly turned the faucet toward the off position. Even the tears had stopped. She didn't say a word, though judging by her reaction, she was floored. Silence entered between us, until she lowered her head, walked out of the room, and closed the door behind her.

I didn't know what to do. My first thought had been to run. Funny thing was that I felt so much better now. This had been the first time in my life I'd been able to talk to someone about what happened to me. I was sure, though, that she'd return with the police in tow. Instead, she walked in, the evidence of her tears still lingering, and placed a bag in my lap. She told me that her gym clothes were inside and that she wanted me to take them, to change.

"How old are you?" she asked.

When I told her I was seventeen, I saw her grip the middle of her stomach and squeeze her eyes as if that would hold back her own tears.

"Do you have someone, some family, that you can go stay with?"

I lied and told her that I had an aunt that lived in New York, and that I was sure she would let me stay with her. She seemed relieved and told me to go and change my clothes before the police saw me, I did.

She gave me a one-way ticket to New York at no charge and her phone number. She even made me promise to call her when I got to New York, to let her know that I had arrived safely. I told her I would but even then, I knew that was probably a lie. That is how I ended up in New York.

○ ◉ ○

# Chapter 5

"The word *love* never was mentioned again in that house and J.K. took it all in as he grew up. He saw the power of his dad, the lack of it by his mother and in between it all he learned one thing: it was okay to never show emotion."

○ ◉ ○

# Even a Beast Has a Beginning

They say when he was born, his brown, curly hair was so perfect that every nurse on the floor wanted to run her hands through it. And it was said, that looking into his blue eyes was like seeing the most beautiful ocean in the world. That's what they said when Jonathan Creek came into the world.

His mother, Sarah Ann Creek was twenty-one then, and having a child had been nowhere in her plans for life. While the rest of the world appeared to be caught in the wave of what was later termed the era of hippy music and sunflowers, Sarah Ann Creek had made another list for her life. The first thing on it was marriage, but not just any marriage. It would be a marriage that didn't revolve solely on love, not that she didn't believe in it.

She found the term to be associated with the fairytales of young pig-tailed girls, more so than what she deemed to be actual reality. She never cared about the things her parents had tried so often to instill into her head. She didn't believe in stories of white knights or the ones of the handsome and charming prince. She never cared for either of those things. She preferred to always live in the realm of reality; that was her comfort zone.

She married Kenneth Creek, whose family owned the Bay & Creek Vineyards up in California. While children, hippy music, and sunflowers, stayed for a moment, on her list of fairytales.

In fact, as soon Kenneth had begun to hint at the very concept of children, shortly after their three-year anniversary, she'd rushed off to see a doctor about birth control. She was sure that would keep the fairytales at bay.

Sarah Ann Creek was what most women dreamed of becoming. Even at seventy her skin was the color of an olive, her long auburn hair flowed in just the right amount of curls, hanging just in the middle of her lean back.

She was smart and funny and could drink a can of beer quicker than a man, while maintaining her womanly demeanor. She loved sports, just about any kind, but when it came to numbers, she was what some people considered a genius. In fact, doing the books for the Creeks her senior year in high school was how she met Kenneth.

Kenneth Creek was just an inch over six feet and when he stood up straight, he had the broadest shoulders you'd ever seen. His green eyes were like those of a cat, some even called them captivating. But on the other hand, he offered not much else. His straight hair was often swooped in the front and slicked back on each of the sides. He had the kind of smile you didn't remember, and the confidence, you never forgot.

To be honest, many people felt that when the wedding had been announced that the *m* word: money was the dominating force behind the wedding invitation. Neither of them cared.

From the time they met, he knew that Sarah wasn't with him for his looks. Rather, everyone knew that Sarah, even in high school, was a woman who knew a brilliant man when she saw one—and Kenneth Creek was as smart as they came.

In fact, when they graduated from high school together, his plan was to go into real estate not wine making. He wanted nothing to do with his parents' business, but wanted to make his fortune on the back of his own name. And that was what Sarah loved most about Kenneth: his ambition. It fit perfectly in her plans of reality.

They didn't date long. The summer after their high-school graduation, Kenneth asked for her hand in marriage. The proposal was nothing romantic, nothing to record in the book of proposal history, but it was realistic for her and simple for him.

Kenneth was a man who believed in keeping words, things, and life, simple and to the point. He never beat around the bush as they say.

The wedding was nothing romantic either. It seems that, from the beginning, they both knew their marriage would be centered on business. He was smart and she was good with the books, something he needed to be successful in the world of real estate. And yet somewhere underneath all the red tape, they did in fact love each other.

They left the Windy City and moved into a small one-bedroom apartment in New York. She was seventeen and he was eighteen. Some might have said they were too young to do what they did, too inexperienced and foolish, but to them, that was the challenge of it all.

A month after the move, Kenneth began searching for property that he could buy cheap, renovate, and sell for big bucks. It was a simply plan for making money and one that, within a year, had begun to pay off big time. It seemed he also had a knack for selecting property, that later, would become some of the most popular places in New York to visit.

By year two, Kenneth and Sarah had not only made headline news as the one of the wealthiest younger couples in New York, but also had moved from the small one-bedroom apartment to a five-bedroom estate in upper New York. Everything, it seemed, was going as they had planned.

That is, until the following year, when they were out celebrating their third-year anniversary and Kenneth announced that he felt it was time to have a child.

The very thought of it, burst the big balloon of focusing only on self, that lived inside the head of Sarah. It frightened her down to the very core of what she based her entire existence upon.

Some might call her selfish but she enjoyed living her life. She and Kenneth had the freedom to travel when they wanted, go out to dinner whenever the mood struck, or just sit at home and enjoy the silence. She didn't want any of it to change. Ironically, the very thing she did to prevent that change—go to the doctor to inquire about birth control— was what brought change upon her like a fury.

When Kenneth found out, they say outrage was a calm word for the way he reacted. And the outcome of the situation was that she found herself in a hospital room nine months later, giving birth to a son she never wanted. They named him Jonathan Kenneth Creek—later to become J.K. for short.

For Kenneth, J.K. seemed to complete the perfect picture that was his life; his list. But, for Sarah, her life seemed to burst into thin air. *Poof!* Out came the baby and out the door went her freedom.

And so she became cold and distant, even to J.K. Kenneth thought it was just a phase at first, and everyone agreed with him, telling him that it would just wear off. But after a year of her not even looking at the boy, he knew it was the real thing; and it frightened him.

So he tried giving her everything that money could buy, from expensive jewelry to the best shrink in New York City, but nothing would convince her that her freedom had not vanished. He even went to great lengths to plan trips for just the two of them to assure her, but even he had to admit it was all different.

He found himself caught between loving his wife and trying to be a mother and father to his son, until finally one sad day, she made a fatal decision that ended with just him and J.K. She turned his simple, uncomplicated life, his perfect picture, into something colored with hues of grey. She left him.

He would never forget that day, the day he came home and found all of her things gone. There was no note, no good-bye—only an empty closet. He wondered whether she had even said good-bye to J.K., but deep down he knew the answer to that.

One could say that he became angry, but most would call it going completely mad. He hired only the best P.I. to find her but later as time revealed very quickly and clearly to him, the moment Sarah Ann Creek found out that she was pregnant, she began to plan her exit.

The year prior, she had established a secret account and deposited a certain amount of money into it every month. He never even noticed the small amounts of clothing that she began clearing out of her closet. He'd never caught wind of the fact that her jewelry had slowly disappeared over the last several weeks from their safe.

Only five months after her exit did he learn that she had stashed away over three million of his hard-earned dollars. And when he did, it changed the way Kenneth looked at women forever. Yes, madness had been just the beginning for him. It later consumed even his nightmares.

Two years had passed when the money began to dwindle in her bank account. Her three-bedroom condo cost her over three thousand a month. Her drinking habit probably cost her more. Her lifestyle, well let's just say that it was a mess and then some.

Although in the beginning, she had found her escape to be rejuvenating, the idea of being twenty-two and free to do as she wanted, when she wanted and how she wanted, had excited even her mental capacity.

On the outside, she was living the dream, on the inside, her bubble had popped loud enough that even ones that didn't know her, knew she was in need of help.

Her desire for freedom, she began to realize had cost her too much; way too much. And as hard as she tried not to admit it, the truth went beyond casual denial. She found that the truth always came back and handed her a new version of reality, whether she wanted to accept it or not.

By the time she realized what was happening to her, she'd gotten herself hooked on things that polluted her mind, corrupted her thinking and her ability to reason. So much so, that one day she discovered herself sitting in a park, on a cold worn-out bench, with a full-length mink coat on her and not remembering at all how she got there. She longed to see Kenneth again, but how could she call him now.

Technically, they were still married and she'd always known that he would look for her. She anticipated that and planned accordingly. But now she found herself wondering if he had moved on, dismissing her and her need for freedom. How she wished he was still looking for her, she just might let herself be found.

Then exactly three years to the date of her departure, as she sat in a coffee shop, she spotted him and "that boy" walking into a children's bookstore. Even then she wanted to run to him and beg for his forgiveness, but then she saw J.K.—the reality of what that meant, motherhood, almost made her want to vomit. She knew she was no mother, and frankly, never wanted to be. How could she go back?

She longed for the security that being a wife brought, and therefore longed to claim that role again, but that was it. She knew that Kenneth would expect so much more. He would expect her to put on the mother hat and prance around. That just wasn't in her.

Little did she know that Kenneth had seen her that day, sitting in the front window of the coffee shop, sipping on what he figured was probably her favorite hang-over remedy. He recognized her even behind the dark shades she used to cover her shamefulness. The anger that filled him as he had stood, with J.K. holding his hand ever so tightly, made him want to dash through the congestion of traffic, just so he could slap the smile that resided on her face. J.K. had been the only thing that had held him back. He didn't want his son to witness such a scene.

It took nine months more months after that, but the day came when the P.I. walked into Kenneth's office and handed him all the details of his lost wife's whereabouts. And from that point forward, Kenneth, not only kept up with her life, but became secretly involved in it.

He watched her from a distance through photographs and monthly reports. He knew that she was almost broke; in fact, he was partly responsible for it. Without her knowledge, he brought the building she was living in and increased her rent. He made sure that whatever she got involved in, if it would result in her bank account being depleted, would be at his finger tips.

Yes, Kenneth Creek had crossed the bounds of madness. But he knew that soon the day would come when the clothes and the jewelry would return, and that very soon Sarah would have no choice but to fill the role of mother that she'd run away from. (The "wife" part, however, was still out for questioning.) And yet, *soon*, for him, couldn't be soon enough.

Every day he thought about it, he literally dreamed about it and then one afternoon, as he was sitting in his office reading the morning paper, his office phone rang. It was her.

He had let it ring for almost a minute or two before he answered it. He didn't want it to go into voicemail. As he talked with her, his voice was so slow and deliberate, it were as though he'd rehearsed the conversation a million times and truth be told, he had. It had taken three years, eleven months and twenty-one days for this very moment to arrive, so he was more than ready. He wondered if she was.

"Where have you been Sarah?" He said, with mock soberness.

"I've haven't been far, believe it or not. I couldn't move too far from you, Kenneth."

"Why did you leave?" Knowing the reason already, he almost had to kick himself to keep his temper in check as he asked.

"I know you won't understand Kenneth, but it was all just too much for me.

I needed my freedom and I thought it had all been taken away from me, but Kenneth, I still love you."

"You do?" He figured about half of that was truth and the other half was something else.

Yet, she said, "Yes, I do."

"I don't know how to respond to that," he said. He knew how he wanted to respond, though. He knew that he wanted to tell her to really get lost this time and then slam the phone down, but then his plan for the past three-plus years would all be in vain. He wouldn't let his emotions get in the way of that. Not now, now that he was just at the beginning of it all.

"Kenneth, I want to meet. Can we have dinner somewhere?"

"I don't know Sarah." He said this smiling ever slightly behind his words.

"Look Kenneth, I know that I caused you a great deal of pain. I can't apologize for that, I know it won't change matters. I do, however, want you to hear me out, to understand my side of things."

He wanted to say so many things to her just then but it was not in the rehearsed script that he had so many times played over and over in his head. So he took a deep breath, and arranged for a car to pick her up.

When the conversation ended and the receiver was placed back on the hook, Kenneth leaned back, and a smirk of a smile slowly crept across his face. The game was just beginning.

Over the next six months, he entered into the next level of his game. The game of "letting" her win him back.

However, as much as he had enjoyed it while it lasted, he knew that it was time to pull out his final card and lay down the rules of return. It was time to end the game on that level, for now.

At first, she just looked at him blankly, as he spoke to her, but he knew that in the end she would give in. He was never wrong about these matters. Kenneth Creek knew how to play the game and win. It was why he was in real estate.

J.K. got a mother, the clothes were returned, the jewelry replaced, the bank account closed, and the little money that had been left, withdrawn and deposited into their son's account. The drinking stopped and so did every other habit she had gotten into.

Kenneth had played the game well and Sarah knew it. In the end, she still lost what she tried so hard to hold on to, her freedom.

The wife part of the matter, however, was forever removed off the table. He knew that he didn't want her back for that reason.

The word *love* never was mentioned again in that house and J.K. took it all in as he grew up. He saw the power of his dad, the lack of it by his mother and in between it all he learned one thing: never show emotion. That lesson he learned very well from each of them. Later, however, it became more apparent in his mother.

○ ◉ ○

# Chapter 6

"What is a moment? Some would say that a moment
is a tiny piece of time, a fraction of something that you
once longed for but then realized that it was gone,
just like that; a moment. My moment probably
should have never been."

⊙◉⊙

# What Is a Moment

I felt like jumping off the bus with joy as soon as the bus driver said, "Welcome to New York!" I could almost taste freedom now. It was like the perfect piece of milk chocolate melting on my tongue. I wanted to savor it, make it last forever.

But then a strange fear, a familiar enemy, swept by me. It was reality, back again to laugh in my face, remind me of its existence and the reality of my situation.

There I was in New York, young, dumb and stupid. I had no job, no skills and no place to live. But once I stepped off the bus, placed both feet on the hot pavement, the fear subsided. I stared at my enemy reality and gave it a couple of slaps for messing with me. Yes, I thought for the moment that I was tough. Seconds later I realized, that I would kill to have that moment back again.

What is a moment? Some would say that a moment is a tiny piece of time, a fraction of something that you once longed for but then realized that it was gone, just like that; a moment.

My moment probably should have never been. It's funny when you think about it; all we have in life are a bunch of moments. This fact became the reason why I felt determined not to live for the moment, as the saying goes, but to allow the moment to live through me, to breathe life back into my voice, to give me a reason to sing again.

With the pavement still burning through the soles of my shoes and the breath of determination giving me a renewed sense of zeal, I realized that young, dumb and stupid, didn't belong in New York. So, I left those qualities in that moment, and walked away from them.

As I began my approach onto the busy streets of New York, I thought that walking away from that moment, those qualities or colors that were trying to get in my box was the right thing to do. They were trying to steal my new moments. In fact, I had determined that it was time to get a new box of colors.

Years later, a young reporter once asked me what made me famous. Was it my voice, or was it just the right moment for me. How funny that question was to me at the time, but as I think about it now, I realize how right of a question it turned out to be. So I am going to do you a favor, I am going to tell you about the color of the crayon box that made me take a deep breath and sing.

As I watched the bus fade away, I walked down a street I didn't know the name of, to a place I had never been, through a set of doors that to this very day I wish I had never opened, and into a life that lasted more than I care to think about. It was called, The Skinny.

The Skinny belonged to a man named Big Daddy Fred. He got the name not because of his height but because of his voice. Big Daddy Fred could do more than blow his pipes into something sensual; he could make your toes curl when he opened his mouth to sing.

When I first heard him, I admit I was ready to fall off my chair and just grovel at his feet—and stay there, forever. To this day I will tell you this; that man could *sing*!

Some wonder why Big Daddy Fred didn't make it to the top, but the answer is simple, and rather sad. Big Daddy Fred was as dark as dark could get for a black man, and the world, it seemed at the time wasn't ready for that.

Many singers had come and gone out of his place, leaving him for bigger and better venues; some even becoming stars. But he didn't seem to mind that he never got his shot at what was considered stardom, because he got everything else he wanted, and without all the fancy lights and stars in the sky. How? He was smart, loud and just plain mean!

He didn't care about you, your problems or your mama's problems. He only cared about the reaction people got from hearing great music. It always meant getting his favorite thing from them: money. Money was Big Daddy Fred's claim to fame; he had more of it than anyone knew. Although to look at him, you'd swear he was broker than a doorman.

When I first walked into The Skinny, the smoke alone could have killed me. If I had known what I learned later about the place, I wished that the smoke had. Picture this scene, if you will. Close your eyes and image a place filled with smoke so thick that you can barely make out the faces sitting at the tables.

You hear the live band, only you can't see them. You look up at the lights that scan the tops of the puffs of smoke to find the bar, and then you realize its right next to you.

The floor feels like it's submerged in puddles of water underneath your feet, because it's so nasty. And the only real movement you can pick out is the one waitress you see, and that is only because she is standing just a few feet from you, screaming to the top of her lungs. That, my friend, was how it was every night at The Skinny.

The Skinny was in a world by itself, once you were inside.   Outside the world had moved into the era of boy band groups and big hair. Inside The Skinny, Jazz was always the flavor. People flocked to get into The Skinny just to listen to the blow of the horn, the rhythm of the saxophone, the beat of the drum.

There was one thing that I loved about that place, and I will only admit this just this once; it was the live band. Man, could they play.  No one could play the way they could then. But even their playing hardly made up for the nasty attitudes they wore once the lights went on and the music stopped.

I hated everything else, I mean downright loathed it! As always, reality reminded me that I needed money and a place to lay my head. The Skinny suited both of those purposes.

I want to take a few steps back and tell you about my first encounter with Big Daddy Fred. You see, I had been there for awhile, "taking it all in" as they say, when I'd felt his heavy hand upon my shoulder. The suddenness of his touch made my heart fall to the floor with such loudness that I was sure, positive that everyone heard it. He stood behind me for quite awhile with his hand on my shoulder. I had found it strange and rather uncomfortable.

His speaking voice was deep, but still had smoothness to it. I admit that I imagined him to be tall and handsome, so much so, that I allowed this to play inside my head for a moment. Reality however revealed something quite different once the lights came on and I turned around to face him.

It was hard for me to believe, but standing in front of me, was this short, fat, bald man staring me in the face with a grin that screamed "I am the boss." There went my moment.

He said, "You're a little young to be in a joint like this, aren't you girlie?"

Okay, the girlie part had made me want to just spit in his face, but instead I forced a smile, looked him straight in the eye and just said, "This girlie needs a job." I had to play the 'girlie' role. Broke and no place to sleep, meant be whatever color the situation deemed. I had to reach deep in my box.

He didn't ask any questions, didn't care to hear my story or where I came from. Nothing but a moment stood between us, and within a split second, even that moment went. He walked away, screaming at a girl who looked younger than I was to show me the ropes. Her name was Misty.

Misty was a light-skinned woman, tall in appearance, slender where needed and had hair that stopped just in the mid-part of her back. She walked over to me, looked me up and down and then turned around. That was it. It's funny how, in a moment, you can go from bad to downright in the dumps. My moment as The Skinny had begun.

My life at The Skinny, however, lasted too long. It was mixed with people who never heard you and music that at times, I never got a chance to hear. One of those people was Charles T. Williams, and man, when I tell you he was beautiful, it was the truth that set my heart in motion.

However, before I go into the details of how I met Charles T. Williams, I need to stay on Big Fred for a moment.

I had been at The Skinny for about six months, working day and night. Big Fred had let me sleep in the back until I could save enough money to pay rent in one of the dumps around the corner.

It was the only kind thing he had even done for me, if one could call it kind. With the hours that I put in, I should have been able to afford to buy a whole apartment building, but Big Fred, remember I told you, was in love with the *m* word, and he found it hard to let go of. It didn't help matters that he knew I had nowhere else to go. Here's a point that you might find somewhat ironic, I remember the first night I laid my head upon that cot in the back that had never been washed, and thought that freedom had finally found me.

The night Charles T. Williams came in, though, I was at the point of thinking that perhaps being raped week after week had been better than being at The Skinny. I had missed having a real bed to sleep in, and a bathtub to soak in, one that allowed my troubles to float down the drain and into a world where no one cared. What I would have given for a real shower instead of barely having enough time and privacy to wash up in the women's restroom each day.

It was at this point in my life, that I realized I must be careful of what I wish for, and even more cautious of men who claim they can make all your wishes come true. This fact now brings me back around to the subject of Charles. From his brown eyes to the tip of the perfectly polished black leather shoes he had on the first time I saw him, everything about him was fine. (make 1 paragraph)Beyond fine, he was like cotton candy, the kind that sits in your mouth and lingers for a moment just before it finally melts, and you can feel it slide down your throat and land in the soft spot of your stomach.

*Okay*, where was I? *Oh yes*, speaking about Mr. Williams as he called himself. That right there should have lit rockets off in my head, but the moment of "young and dumb" had found me again, and I, for my part, welcomed them back with open arms.

Actually, open arms, doesn't quite help to get the sense of what I'm talking about. Let's say that he could tell me to jump, and I would say something like, "How high do you want me to go, in which direction and for how long?" I think you get the point.

Conversation between Charles and I saw it's beginning, when Big Fred walked up to me and said, "Girlie, are you going to get him a drink?" You know that expression "a cat got your tongue?" Well for me, the whole block of them had chipped in. I found myself looking at a man that was to me perfect in every sense of the word. He was also, however, the perfect picture of a spider, eyeing its prey before the catch. Mr. Williams had me caught in his web with just his smile. Getting back to describing the conversation between Charles and myselftook awhile, but, finally I'd opened my mouth to say, "What can I get you sir?"

That was all I could manage to utter, as I looked down at the shine of his perfectly polished black leather shoes.

For a moment, I swear I saw a reflection of our wedding day in them shoes, and found myself smiling when I finally had the courage to look into his brown eyes. When he returned the look, I could barely keep myself from hitting the floor.

You know, it's funny how one decision starts the clock turning for every other choice in life. You begin to wonder, if you had just made one decision differently, which way the clock would have turned, left or right?

It's true, I suppose, that one decision can either move you forward or backward. Well, I made the decision to bring that man a cold beer and then I made the decision to go out with him. Which way did my clock turn?

Let me answer that one for you, it turned down the aisle, to the left and detoured straight onto the road of nonsense. Funny isn't? Not really, it hurt.

How do you love such a man? Do you feed him soft candy canes, or dance for him in the rain? Do you tell him he's a man and that his soft touch feels as smooth as the sand that flows between your fingertips? Does he even hear the words that glide off your lips? Does he listen with his heart instead of with his ears? How do you love such a man? Do you clothe him with your love; embrace him with your song?

Do you whisper ever so lightly, "love me in the summer and kiss me in the night, hold me in the fall and shelter me through it all just before the roses begin to fall?" How do you love a man, when he says to you, there is no love from this heart, only a moment, that you can never start? How long will it last? Your heart is afraid to ask. How do you walk out the door, away from something you've never had before? Can you love such a man, really?

For six months more, I stared at those shinny black shoes. You know, I feel like telling you everything, right down to the tiniest detail about those six months, but I won't. I will only tell you this, because it speaks to a truth that never changes: you know how it is when you meet someone who offers you just a little more than life but then delivers on nothing? What happens?

You marry him and then reality steps in and says "hello" again. Mr. Williams never listened to me and never cared one dime about me, until the day I opened my mouth and began to sing.

The way it happened was like a whirlwind. He flew into the house one day, as I was in our tiny kitchen cleaning up the mess he always forgot he made. I was so angry at the situation that something inside me wanted to let it come out, so I began to sing. It had been a long time, too long. I didn't even see him standing there, but when I turned around trying to avoid the whiff of some woman's cheap perfume looming in the air, I saw him staring at me like he had seen me for the first time.

Now this next statement will probably make you want to just reach and touch me across the face real hard, but I admit that seeing him look at me like that, made me want to love him for the both of us. Downright crazy, I know, but when you have never had the love of a man that you love, let's just say that a look like that can cover over so many empty promises.

The words that came off the lips of my husband for the first time, made me want to sing to the universe, if I could.

I truthfully thought for a moment, perhaps it was more like a split of a split second—that I had found the way to his heart. My voice would be the juice that started the ignition that had never felt the key turn it before. This thought, had pushed me into a new realm of reality. Unfortunately, it was a thought that lasted only for a moment and a reality that never became anything more than a second.

Before I knew it, before I even got a chance to enjoy my moment, he had hurled me down to The Skinny, thrown me upon the floor, and told me to sing like I was singing to a man who loved me. They say words never really hurt you; I say words can downright kill you. The microphone man introduced me as Jazzmyne, the Jazz singer. This is the song that I sang.

*I closed my eyes to you my love, and felt the love inside. I took a breath, and felt the wind fly over me. Ever so gently, it seems. I looked into your eyes and saw the world as it was meant to be. I saw a man, a woman, staring into that never ending sunset. I reached out, I felt the wind and it liked me. It liked me looking at you. It liked me loving you. I reached out once again, and stroked the softness of your smile. I touched the tip*

*of your laugh and wondered how long it would last.*
*Was it just like a melody, or was it like the wind, that*
*blew just beneath the sea, for what seemed an eternity?*
*I waited, I waited my love. I waited for your touch. I*
*waited for your caress. I waited for your love, the love*
*that never seemed to reach me.*

*I kept reaching for it, kept screaming for it. Calling*
*out to it, come and touch me. My heart is open, my*
*love is waiting. Come to me. Your love never an-*
*swered. It never sought, not even for a moment, the*
*love that was glowing inside my heart."*

The wind stopped and I open my eyes. I remember
feeling the tears stroll down my cheeks, very much as they
are doing now. You know; I didn't care about the applause.
I didn't care what my performance might have meant or
done for me. All that I cared about, I saw hutched in a
corner, whispering something into an ear that was obviously wasn't mine. Having watched her response, I wished it
had of been mine, should have been mine, so I cried and
cried again.

That moment, for me was not a box of milk chocolates. It certainly wasn't like the fresh smelling roses, it should have been. Life, to me was never sweet, sometimes bitter, and well, often I just wanted to throw the box away and eat ice cream.

When I stepped off the stage, he took no note. He only seemed to notice the applause. It didn't shock me.

Have you even seen a scene like this: the ever-so-loving husband, proud and glowing with praise for his wife as he comes over to congratulate her on her accomplishment? His chest is stuck out because he just can't believe that she once said, "I do." Can you picture it? It's downright beautiful, isn't it? The problem, however, was that it never happened to me.

It was at this point of the narration that I stopped. I waited for some response. I received nothing. I watched as my son got up and walked toward my office door. I watched as he put his hand on the knob, I could see just a tiny reflection of his strength in his grip. He stops and stares toward the door for a second. I think he's about to speak, about to utter a word.

He doesn't say a thing. It angers me. He simply opens the door, walks down the hall and out the door of my house, the one he feels he should have grown up in. I realize then, that he wasn't really listening to my story. I get up and walk over toward the window; I pull back the curtain and lean my head against the wall. I sigh. I watch him as he stands on the covered porch he never got a chance to play on and I see him raise his hands to his eyes. Could it be?

I stand, still holding back the curtain, watching my son cry. That is how we ended our first meeting, our first moment.

◯ ⦿ ◯

# Chapter 7

"Pretend for a moment that I didn't have a son.

Then pretend for a moment that one day the words

'I love you' would fall off his tongue."

**o ⊙ o**

# Pretend For a Moment

The sun was hovering behind the clouds as if it needed a reason to come out. Perhaps it was playing with me, knowing that if it showed its brilliant head, I would have to once again look into the eyes of my son and say things that I wished I didn't have to, words I could barely get off my lips. I would have liked to think that the sun was hovering as a way to say, "Today, I think I'll let it stay dark for Jazzy's sake." I would have liked to think that.

It was just after six in the morning, as I lay there in my ivory bed, covered with crème silk sheets and plush goose-down pillows. I stared at the linen robe that I had made for myself a few months ago, still hanging on my bathroom door in plastic.

I thought about the glass of water that always sat on my hand-carved desk, which was imported from some country I honestly can't remember now. I bet he just wanted to drop a pill in that water. Then he could have all of this. I laughed at that, only because I know it's not true but that's the point of pretend. It's been a long time since I've heard myself laugh. One might think that with the fame and fortune I've cultivated over the years, I could pay someone to make me laugh, but you know real laughter can't be bought; it can only be felt.

I heard the phone ring and then suddenly stop. I didn't reach for the one in my bedroom. I already know that someone on the staff would quickly pick up the receiver so as not to disturb me. I do, however, strain to hear the faint whisper, "I will give her the message." I hear a tap at my door, ever so light and soft, and I'm reminded that while money can't buy real laughter, it can buy morning peace, if only for a second or two. Perhaps if I'd dug deeper into my bank account, I could've gotten a whole ten minutes.

"Your guest would like to arrive at ten o'clock to continue his visit," my help said, peeking through a crack in the door.

I nodded slightly and leaned my head back, trying to pretend that I was okay with that. Pretend. Now there is a word that the world never has to teach you. After all, pretending is not something you develop. When you're young and hear it for the first time, you don't stop and wonder what it means. And then as you grow older, it seems, you slowly but almost certainly become the very essence of it. You start by pretending to like things such as vegetables and milk, and then you move into the more serious type of pretending. You start pretending that you are loved, pretending someone cares for you, pretending someone wants to hold you each and every day, pretending that you love them and want to do the same, pretending to want to live or even to care.

Now, pretend for a moment that I didn't have a son. Then pretend for a moment that one day the words "I love you" would fall off his tongue. Pretend for a moment that I would one day look into a mirror and not see my past. Pretend for a moment that my name wasn't

Jazzmyne, the want-to-be mother of the never-to-be son. You see, pretending is easy. Reality, however, doesn't pretend; it becomes.

I can't tell you that when I heard the doorbell ring, I ran with open arms. I can't even say a small smile crossed my face when I saw him slide out of his new Jaguar, as though telling me that *his* money bought him that. I had begun to get the impression that he wanted to make sure that I knew that he too, had money. I wasn't sure why this was so important to him, but it was obvious by the way that he dressed that he was trying to make a statement. I wanted to tell him that my money could have purchased that car, along with his wardrobe, all his shoes, every tie and cufflink, his entire livelihood for that matter, without so much as a sweat.

And though I never let it slide off my tongue, only because I knew he had worked hard to get all of it, I felt myself going back to my old self, the part of me that never had a son. The part of me that suspected this man was now coming to me like every other man had, just trying to make a name from my fame. So I had to catch myself, put my thoughts in check.

As he entered my room, there was something different about him, some strange mannerism that made me nervous. I just looked him in the eye and tried not to blink. He walked over and put an envelope in my hands. As I opened it, I saw him watching, waiting, wanting to see some type of reaction from me.

But this wasn't the first time I had gotten an envelope containing what I was sure was something from my past, and it probably wasn't the last. I didn't tremble while I opened it, then, certain that it was the same as always—just a gift from someone who wanted to know the person behind the name. For his sake, however, I pretended to open it slowly, and then I pulled out something that felt like newspaper.

When I looked down to see the image on the paper, my heart didn't just skip a beat; I think it flew out the window and ran down the street. It was a picture of him and the beast. I couldn't pretend now, even for a moment. The saying "Never let them see you sweat" became then, for me, something more like "Never let them see you scream."

After a minute, I did finally look up at him, but only to say, "Did you call him Daddy?"

It was a cold, perhaps even harsh thing for me to say, but so very called for. He wanted to play with my feelings, and I wasn't going to let him. How could he bring me a picture of that man, that thing that once called himself my father?

Now I was sure I was back to my old self again, but, honestly, I liked it. It was my old self that convinced me it was time to get over the "mommy thing," which would never happen and just live in that moment.

My response caught him off guard, but he quickly collected himself. Probably an ability he got from me; after all, moment or not, he was still my son.

"Should I have called him Daddy?" he said. "Funny thing. When I first found out about him, I was excited to know that I had family, that I had a history that was finally touchable. Because when you grow up with a family you know you never really belong to, you yearn to just touch your history—just to know that it exists." His eyes bore into me then, as he continued. "But here is where the history thing was cut off—I had myself tested just to be sure, and guess what I found? You already know, don't you?"

I remembered then; the man in the alleyway. I had worked so hard to forget him, and now my own flesh and blood was making me relive yet other nightmare of my youth.

"You already know that your father wasn't *really* my father, don't you? So why don't we both stop playing games here, Mother. I mean, you are my mother, aren't you? Or is that a lie too?"

I stood up and walked over to him. And after my hand quickly reached out to slap the right side of his chin, I didn't say, "Sorry, I didn't mean to do that." Moments are what define you, and this one would define not only me, but us, forever. I opened my mouth to provide a response.

"You want to stop playing games, do you?" I said. "I told you from the beginning that the color of Jazzmyne runs deep. So which color would you like me to reveal now? Which box would you like to pull from, the new one or the old?"

"Mother, please just tell me the truth. Who is my father *really?*"

I stood there in a rage, looking at him, all the while realizing that I'd just heard the word "mother" fall off his lips.

"What is a father anyway?" I asked him. "I had a father once, and look at what he did to me. You want a father? No, what you want is a dream, a fairytale of what you believe to be reality. You envision some man standing in front of you with open arms, telling you how sorry he is for not being there—no different than what you wanted from me."

"No, Mother." His voice immediately calmed. "I just want to know where I came from. I want to be able to tell my children how far they are rooted. They have a right to know. I can't keep telling them I have no past. I have a right to know."

He sighed. "I came here today to put all the cards on the table. To stop the mind games and just find out the truth so that I can move on, so that my family can stop seeing me suffer because I can't get over not being wanted and making them feel as if they are not enough for me."

"I can't keep making them feel that the life we have together is not enough. When my children go to color, I want them to be able to use a crayon box made of real history, true history. I want them to know who their father is. I came here not just for me, but for them."

My head began to spin, my throat became dry, and I felt as if my voice was off traveling the world and forgot to catch a flight home. I was losing it. So I turned around and walked out the door of my own room. I walked down the hall and turned the corner, where I found myself standing in front of my office door.

I went in and rushed to my desk drawer, from which I pulled out my own yellow envelope, the one with the picture of my son and his children. I opened it. And when I looked into the eyes of his children, I began to cry. I was really starting to hate crying. Every tear was like a reminder of all the ugly colors that had come into my life and overstayed their welcome.

Still, his footsteps were coming down the hallway, fast and with a purpose. He wasn't going to let it be.

Have you ever felt like cussing? Well that's how I felt at that moment, but I knew it wouldn't help me hide my tears from him. So when I looked up and saw him standing in the doorway, watching me, all I could do was sit, letting the tears soak into my cheeks. I couldn't hide them, so I didn't try.

And, right then, it seemed as though we both just needed to pretend this moment never happened, that our story would have a happy ending.

Finally, he said, "You knew, didn't you?"

"Yes."

"How long have you known?"

I didn't know how to answer that question. I didn't know if I even wanted to answer that question. What I did know is that, for the moment, I just wanted him to leave, to get out of my house and honestly, out of my life. I wanted to go back to the days when I would just sit here at my desk and read the reports that I would receive from the P.I. and look at the pictures I had of him, of his children, of his life.

I wanted to go back to the moments when I could pretend that they were all coming to see me. Coming to see Grandma, only I would never allow them to call me that. I had even made up a name for them to call me by. I would allow something simple like, "Nana." I wanted to pretend that I was the perfect grandmother, buying presents and showering them with all the things they ever wanted. I wanted to pretend I had a family, and that I too, was deeply rooted.

But now all I could do was sigh. "It doesn't matter how long."

"How long has it been?" he said again.

I tried to act as if I didn't hear him, but then said, "Why do you want to know?"

"How long?!"

That reaction, of course, caught my attention, and it demanded an equal response. So I looked him not just in the eye—oh no—I wanted my response to go even deeper than that. I needed to get close enough to him to feel his breath and look into his very soul. Yes, this response needed to be something of utter substance. The tears had dried, the pretending had stopped, and reality now stood between us.

"I know you feel you have a right to raise your voice," I said, very calmly, "feeling your emotions tug on that cord in you that seems to demand a response from me. But let me assure you that not now, not tomorrow, and not ever will you ever get a response from me using a tone of voice like that."

"You think you have rights because you found out something, something you consider to be a lie, so I will give you this moment. Please, have a seat."

Calming down, then, he situated himself in a chair by the window. I, however, remained on my feet. I started again. No narration—this required a direct conversation.

"When I told you there are many shades of Jazzmyne, I wasn't being comical. Rather, I was being honest. And here is some more honesty for you, son—because yes, you are indeed that: my son."

"The man in your picture—that beast—did rape me; just as I told you, not even a detail of that was a lie. But there was one night I thought to be more of a nightmare than I was already in. I was coming home from school—running home was more like it, because the beast always got suspicious if I was ever even a second late and I was late that night. I had stayed after school trying to just get some peace in the library and had lost track of time."

"When I realized how late it was, I decided to take a shortcut. I went through the alleyway, when a man grabbed me and threw me behind a dumpster and began to . . . well . . . I won't go into the details. But in the end, let's just say the beast wasn't the only one to take my fairytales away."

"When I got home that day, he was there and saw my torn clothes. I tried to explain what happened, but he didn't believe me. He called me names and started to hit me."

"So, you see, when I realized I was pregnant, I didn't even think that you weren't his. All these years I thought . . . all these years, I was haunted by the thought that I had given birth to my father's child. Now I understand why he was so angry when you were born. Even now, when I look at you, I can't believe it—you look so much like him and yet you don't. The way you twitch your eyes upward or the way you run your hands through your brown curly hair. I was convinced you were his."

"Is that the truth?" he said, without even a pause.

"Yes, it is the truth. I was raped by a white man in an alleyway coming home from school."

"I'm sorry, I didn't know. I thought you were lying to me."

"To be honest, I am glad that what I told you wasn't all truth. I'm glad to know that you aren't his. But . . . now it's your turn to tell me something." I held up the picture of my son and the beast. "Did *he* tell you the truth? Did he tell you that he took life from me?"

"Yes. It is how I found you."

Have you ever watched someone tell you something and it seems like it's in slow motion, or maybe even in a dream? You pretend for a split second that perhaps you heard them incorrectly. And then you stand there with that dumbfounded look and wonder whether you heard them at all. Yes, that was me and so now it was my turn to sit.

As I did, I remember glancing at a mirror across the room and seeing yet another image of my son: that of a man, someone who was no longer a child. I know you're probably saying, "Enough of the 'my son' drama," but I can't help it. Some moments just bring that hint of pretend, that touch of fantasy and right then, I needed to have one of those.

I turned to him and heard the word "please" fall slowly off my lips. But this time, it was my turn to listen.

# Chapter 8

"You might say that was the day when my history started to lay itself out, like a jigsaw puzzle. It had so many pieces spread out that, to this very moment, has driven me downright mad trying to put together."

# ○ ◉ ○

# Pieces Of a Puzzle

"I guess you could say that life for me began at two or three" he began, staring directly at me as he spoke. I sat up, straight in my chair. I wanted him to know that he had my full attention, that I was listening. "At least that is as far back as I can really remember beginning my life with them. They were not at all like the other parents I would see at school, picking up their children or attending school functions. They were very much different, in every way imaginable.

"For one, they were much older and they never touched—barely even spoke. Looking back at their interaction with one another, I would say that marriage, for each

117

of them, was something that was stated only on a piece of paper. To say they loved each other would probably be stretching the word "love" to new limits. There were moments, however, when I was convinced that there had been a time when it thrived."

"They made it no secret that I had been adopted. The woman, he meant for me to call mother, always made sure that fact was engrained in my head. He, however, seemed to really love having me in the home, I think it brought back memories that he never discussed. When he wasn't around, if I needed to speak, she would make me call her Mrs. C."

"For thirteen years, I was more of a resident in their massive home than anything else. Conversation was on an 'only-when-needed basis.' I was provided with plenty of clothes, food, shelter, and not to mention a top-of-the line education. In a sense, I owe them for that. I would however, had preferred some form of human touch, a laugh every now and then. It would have been nice to get just a speck of emotion from her, an encouraging father-son talk from him or just something that said they knew I existed. I never asked for love, I was sure they weren't capable of providing it."

"I believe I had just turned one, when I officially became the son of Kenneth and Sarah Ann Creek.

"Then one day I was in class, when the principle came to the door and asked that I be excused. I was told that they were killed instantly in a car accident."

"Did I cry? Not necessarily for her, maybe a little for him. I know now that I should have forced the conversation, forced the emotions and demanded that they sit back, take note and show me some love."

"You might say that was the day when my history started to lay itself out, like a jigsaw puzzle. It had so many pieces spread out that, to this very moment, has driven me downright mad trying to put together."

"It was that day that paved the way to my next journey and eventually, to a time when I would be standing in front of you, begging for more pieces. For the next five years I was looked after by the man we both know, a man that had the same name as I did, Jonathan Creek."

"It was rather strange when he and Imet. It was almost as if he had known who I was, way before I knew he existed. The day Kenneth and Sarah died, he walked into their home as if it were just a day ago that he'd left. It's still pretty freaky in my mind, when I take the time to meditate and ponder how it all went down."

"I remember the long drive home from school. I remember the butler ushering me into Kenneth's office for the first time, as I'd never been allowed to go in there before. It was the first time I'd seen a picture of him. Sitting on the mantle, just over the fireplace, were pictures of this young boy who looked liked me."

"I can't go into detail of the emotions that raced through me as I stared at those pictures. Wondering why there was such a strong resemblance between him and I. Wondering if he and I were brothers."

"That perhaps, Kenneth and Sarah had played some cruel, sick joke on me. Making me think I had been adopted, all the while, knowing, they were my real parents. I didn't put the notion past them. I remember feeling my heart rejoice at that thought, for a moment. But I didn't allow it to go off on a tangent."

"I did however, allow those feeling to stir in me a desire to try and put the pieces together. Even now as I stand here, staring at you mother, I still have that desire."

"I was holding one of his pictures in my hands, when he walked into my life. He was much older, but I knew it was him. The moment he sat down, I looked him in the eye and said, 'Are you my brother?' This weird sought of smile came upon his face, and he said, 'You could say something to that effect.' That was it. That was all the information I got out of him at that time. I felt cheated, robbed of a piece of the puzzle I knew he could give me."

"It took a couple of weeks and the execution of the will before he moved into the house with me. He, of course, had inherited just about everything, but I was surprised to hear it came with strings—meaning that unless he agreed to raise me until I was eighteen, he got nothing. A thought entered my mind then, perhaps, they did care. I didn't dwell on it."

"It appeared that my education was included in the list of strings—as long as I remained in school, he had to pay for it."

"At twenty-one, I would also inherit a small apartment that Kenneth and Sarah had once lived in, an undisclosed sum of money until that time and one of the cars. It became clear to me, what really was the cruel and sick joke they played on me."

"I felt as if I had been sold, passed on from one hand that didn't want me to another. It was a rough feeling to overcome, even for a boy at my age then. You know, when the attorney told Jonathan and I all of this, he wasn't surprised. He didn't even flinch, just got up when it was done. Life, for the two of us, had begun."

"For the next two years, I barely saw him; he came and went so much. He kept Kenneth's office locked and his bedroom door locked. He would never allow me to get a question in when he was at home, and the little conversation we did manage to have would lead only to more questions, more pieces of the puzzle that just didn't seem to fit."

"I often felt like I had nowhere to turn. Every corner lead to a dead end until one day, at the age of fifteen, I finally got a small piece of the puzzle to fit."

"He had gone out one night in such a hurry that he'd forgotten to lock his bedroom door. I felt like a kid in a candy store that had never been in one before. I was so nervous and excited at the same time...hoping to find something and yet scared to death that I would."

"I did, find something. Way in the back of his closet, tucked under the piles of junk, was a box overflowing with pictures and newspaper clippings. I fumbled through them for a while, not sure of what I was looking at, until I found a picture album of a young girl. The inside cover said 'Daddy's little girl, Naya Moná Creek.'"

"There were tons of pictures of you as a child. Most of them with him, but then there was one picture of your mother holding you. I looked hard at that picture of you and her, trying to imagine what she was thinking as she was looking down at you. She had this sad look on her face."

As he spoke, I was so caught up in the moment, so intent on hearing and dreading the drop of the ball I felt was coming, I didn't notice his pause. It was only when he turned toward me, that I caught wind of the silence. His look was intense, his emotions running on high and his thoughts focused on his next statement. It was as if he were searching, scanning the colors in my box. Then he reached into my heart, picked out one and said, "Life isn't supposed to be like a puzzle with so many pieces that you can't make them fit. I saw pictures of you on stage, you were so young….you looked so happy, so at peace."

"I could tell just from the pictures that you were born to sing. I didn't need the newspaper clippings that he had of you, to tell me that. You know what I wished for at that very moment? I remember it so well, I wished that I could meet you and find the peace that you clearly had in those pictures. Peace was like my fairytale, and how I longed for a happy ending."

"You think, boys, men, don't believe in fairytales? None, of course would admit it out loud for the world to hear. But inside, inside their box of colors, there's that one color that still believes in the 'once upon a time' stories that his mother told. Too bad, you weren't there to tell me mine. Guess I'm thankful for an imagination."

"Now, even now as I stand before you I still feel like my fairytale hasn't come true. I still feel that peace is still not a part of me."

"Why mother? Why can't I have the peace that you had once upon a time? I hate him, I hate you, I hate what he did to me, I hate what you did to me and still are doing to me! I need peace mother. I just need to know…. what

color is Jazzmyne? I feel like you haven't told me all of it,
like you're only opening half of the box."

○ ◉ ○

# Chapter 9

"How do you give your child peace when it would
cost you so much pain? How do you mend a heart
broken so long ago? Its pieces still buried in places
that can never be found."

○ ◉ ○

# A Mother's Broken Heart

To cry for your own pain, feels like someone sticking you with a needle, constantly. To cry for the pain of your child, feels like someone killing you slowly. To say that my heart broke as my son told me his story, would be putting it mildly.

How do you give your child peace when it would cost you so much pain? How do you mend a heart broken so long ago? Its pieces still buried in places that can never be found.

I was afraid to ask, afraid to know but I had to. I could feel the words spilling from my mouth, and yet I couldn't hear myself speak them, but I knew that I had asked the question: "What did he do to you?" My heart almost couldn't stand to hear the response, but it had to.

"That night," he started, "as I sat looking at your photographs and wondering what true peace felt like, he'd come home. You know, even now I wonder how long he'd been standing there, just watching me and knowing that he had the power to give me a tiny corner of the puzzle. But of course, he didn't."

"Instead, hee waited for me to make eye contact with him, waited for me to ask. So I did. 'Is this your daughter?' I said to him. The silence was like the kind that you hear when you're trying to find the right words to say, but in his case, I think he knew the words I wanted to hear. Which is why when he turned to walk away, I ran after him holding that stupid picture of you in my hand."

"He'd heard me, refused to answer or even stop. And this is the moment, when I began to understand the definition of pain, the essence of hatred and the emotions that followed it."

"Then, there was a brief moment, as he walked down the stairs, he turned and looked at me, and it gave me chills. I don't know why, but as I stood looking down at him, I felt myself asking this man, 'Are you my father?'"

"He didn't answer, didn't even flitch, but only looked at me cold-and-hard-like. And when I saw that same stupid smile that I had seen so many times before, I knew the answer."

"It wasn't exactly the father-and-son moment that I had imagined, nothing like one of those all-time 'if only' scenes I'd created inside my head."

"You know, it was at this point, when hatred began to build in me. Before I had only known the essence of it. Now, however, it was like a ball that's sticky and then you go to roll it in a pile of 'if only' and some 'what if' scenarios. My anger seemed to pick up all sorts of unwanted things."

"For a second, I thought I had finally come to a journey of everlasting peace. I thought that just knowing he was my father would somehow cause all the loneliness to go away."

"I was fifteen years old and still I felt like a child wandering in a forest screaming out to the trees for direction, for the way out, and realizing that they didn't care. For me, that house was like that forest, and he was like the trees refusing to show me the way out."

When he stopped speaking I was captured by the emotions upon his face. The tears were at war inside my heart, my mind fighting to hold back. It was as if I could feel the struggle going on inside of him. His head was down, staring at the floor, unable; it seemed, to look at me. But then he did. How quickly he shifted gears—too quickly, one might say.

"Enough about my twisted dramatic moments of the past," he continued. "Yours are what I'm most interested in. I came here to dig into what will become the colors of my history. So why don't you try to bury me in that box of yours once again."

To say his attitude was cold would be to put it gently. I thought that if I had of had a bucket of water, I'd probably thrown it in his face. Witnessing the difference in his behavior from only a moment before was like watching a before-and-after portrait; and honestly, the "after" just terrified me. It all seemed so well-rehearsed.

I admit, I had to catch my voice, catch it before it went off and knocked him upside his head. I saw him take a few steps back from me as my eyes burned deep into him. All I could manage from my emotions to say to him was, "Let's start digging."

It took a moment, I had to reach deep within myself, deep inside, still struggling to find the words to muster up and start the story again. This time, however, I felt a certain spark ready to pop out of my mouth, a certain renewed sense of energy preparing to fall from my lips. So I closed my eyes and allowed myself to go back in time to dig deep into my crayon box, to mix up the colors that became known as "the meeting"—which in every way put the rest of my life on a path that I wasn't ready for.

# Chapter 10

"Good, because I believe that bright light you're eyeing is worth big dollars for the both of us."

○ ◉ ○

# The Meeting

The Skinny was packed that night. The music was bouncing off the walls and waking up the soul of everyone in there. At this point, I had never seen Mr. Williams, but apparently he had seen me.

"Big Fred, who is that pretty bright light you got working here now?"

"You must be talking about Naya. She's been here a couple of months, came in off the street like they always do. From what I heard from Misty, her daddy is some nutcase who couldn't keep his hands off his daughter. Anyway, I let her stay in the back until she can afford a place of her own."

"Since you're asking, though, why don't we go into my office so that I can run something off you, Mr. Big Investor?"

"You know I'm always ready to talk business" Charles said, chugging a cold beer.

"Good, because I believe that bright light you're eyeing is worth big dollars for the both of us." Even as Big Fred had said it, he was walking out the door. Charles couldn't even get a quick second sip of the beer in his hand, which he had always thought was overpriced.

Big Fred's office was actually just a hidden spot behind the building in the alleyway, where he thought no one could hear him.

"Okay, here's the deal. That bright light can sing like I have never heard a woman sing before, and you and I both know that I have heard a lot of women come in here and blow. But she goes beyond that. I heard her a couple of times as she was getting ready in the bathroom, only I would pretend like I didn't hear a thing. But you know Big Fred has got the gift of hearing lyrics." He even touched his ears to give emphasis to his point.

"Man, her voice is like a sound I can't quite describe—it's like jazz mixed with just the right hint of soul. Only to look at her you'd swear the girl was…well, let's just put it out there, she looks white."

"That's why I know she will be bigger than anything I've had come in here. She can go both ways— blacks will look into her eyes and hear that voice of hers and swear she's one of them, and whites will look at the color of her skin and swear she belongs to them. She's perfect."

As if feeding off the excitement from his own idea, he got a sparkle in his eye. "I've got it! She's got a soulful chocolate voice going on in those lungs of hers, but it's mixed with just the right amount of white chocolate. In fact, if we can pull this thing off, let's call her Jazzmyne."

"Yeah, I hear you," Charles said, "but how do I fit into this money-making scheme of yours?"

"Well, you play the most important part. See, I was thinking that we need something more concrete than a contract to hold the reins on that voice of hers, and seeing that you consider yourself to be such a 'lady's man' I think you should offer her something that will be more binding."

Charles eyes Big Fred. "What do you mean by more binding? What's more binding than getting her to sign an exclusive agreement?"

"You know that never works; women like her need something more." "In fact," he started, as he moved closer toward Charles, "I'll tell you what's more binding than a piece of paper from a man she doesn't know, a piece of paper that represents her heart. You and I both know that saying 'I do' and walking down that aisle is more binding to a woman than any contract could ever be."

He began to really get into the moment now. The excitement of it all had reached its full brim, and was now full of deception.

"You see, we need to hang on to this one. Too many of them have gotten big and run out on me, forgetting it was Big Fred who gave them their start; their lot in life. But I swear to you man, if you were to get in that heart, she'd never want to leave, either of us. And just think, the dollar bills would continue to roll in."

"So, you want me to marry the girl?" Charles said in somewhat disbelief.

"Yes, that's it. I'll sign her to an exclusive deal with me, and you'll play the loving-husband-slash-manager that keeps her exclusive to The Skinny. The heart, my friend, is the way to make this thing work with a woman like that. You know why? Let me tell you. It's because she doesn't know what love feels like. So all you have to do is give her a little taste, and she will be singing jazz like no one's business. You know that's where all jazz is made from, the heart. I don't care if you're a man or a woman. But with women, the heart has to be moved. It has to be touched and driven with emotions, in order for them to produce something each of us can cash in on."

"Are you sure this will work?"

"Look man, I'm sure. I've been watching her for the past couple of months, and that is the way to get her to open that heart of hers and really let out that voice that's trapped inside out." Big Fred touched his own heart and nodded his head, as if it made a difference.

"We got to get in there" he continued, "but we'll give her two more months to let her feel the heat of trying to make a living on her own, and then I'll introduce you and let you do your thing. You cool with that?" He looked for any sign of hesitation. There was none.

"Cool," Charles said. "Let me know when you think she's ready."

"She's almost there, I can tell. Reality is kicking at her door and she's trying to determine if freedom from her past is really worth it. We need you to convince her that it is. Two more months, that's all and she'll be right where I need her to be."

# PART TWO

○ ◉ ○

# Chapter 11

"What is love? Some say if you have to ask, then you've never felt it. I say asking helps you to express it. Helps you to define it not just in your mind but to the point that it blends in with your core and mixes with your insides, and says to him, to this man…'take my heart, it's yours.'"

○ ◉ ○

# What Is Love?

Another year had gone by and another night at The Skinny was upon me. I was standing on the stage like a pro by now, and it was getting tiring. Night after night, I'd find myself looking at so many eager eyes upon me. Looking at that man of mine, hoping that he'd give me a smile or some sense that he too, was listening. Every time I walked into the spotlight; it was like waking up and finding myself still in the nightmare from my sleep. I needed something from him, since love was obviously missing. So I closed my eyes and began to ask.

"What is love? Is it the simple touch of his caress or the breath he breathes upon your neck? Is it the way he reaches inside your soul, digs deep inside your very essence? Does he bring out the sound of your heartjust to make sure it's still in tune? Does he tell you about his dreams? Does he make it seem that they can't exist without you? Does he refine your existence? Define your existence? Breathe life into your kidneys?

Do his words massage your throat, soothe your lungs and bring back the moments when love was all that existed? Do they slide down into your veins, each and every day? What is love? Some say if you have to ask then you've never felt it. I say asking helps you to express it. Helps you to define it not just in your mind but to the point that it blends in with your core and mixes with your insides and says to him, to this man…take my heart, it's yours.

Well, whatever love is, I needed it. I needed emotions, touches, caresses and feelings that go beyond the obvious. I needed him right at that moment to whisper something in my ear that would soak down to the pit of my stomach and slide out to through the tip of my toes and make me beg for more.

It had to be real; it had to be smooth. It had to be a love that would never make me ask that question from the past: what is love?

As usual, by the time I stepped off the stage, I couldn't even look at him. I didn't care about the applause or the fans that came up to me to thank me or tell me how much they liked the show. Something inside me at that point in my life had slowly begun to snap and not only did I not know how to turn it off; I wasn't sure I wanted to.

"Jazzmyne." A man in the audience was behind me, trying to get my attention. "I think that's what I heard them announce you as. Is that correct?"

"It depends—who are you?" I was in such a foul mood that I didn't even look up at the man, who had rushed up and was now walking next to me.

"My name is Daniel Cooper, and I own a live jazz band called The Coopers. Anyway, we've been looking for a female singer and well, after hearing you tonight, I think you're just what we've been looking for."

"That's nice, but I'm not interested and frankly, Mr. Cooper, I'm not sure after tonight that I will ever be interested in singing again."

"Of course you don't mean that?"

Thing is, I really did. I was so tired of feeling like I felt night after night. I couldn't take it anymore and as I squinted through the smog and saw him slouching in a corner with another woman, I knew I couldn't take him anymore. The tears were already sliding down my cheeks. So I just walked away from Mr. Cooper and out into the alleyway. I leaned my head on the cold brick wall, slipped out of my shoes, and as I looked down at the wedding band on my left hand, I began to cry like there was no tomorrow. And at that moment, for me, there wasn't.

"Jazzmyne, you okay?" said a woman's voice behind me. I turned and saw Misty.

"I'm just tired, Misty." It was a response that was more than reality; no, it was the dead, slap–in-your-face truth.

"Tired of The Skinny or tired of him?" Misty said, holding a beer that needed to go to a customer in her hand.

"You know, you'd better get back in there, you know how Big Fred gets when 'his girls' aren't moving the drinks fast enough. To him, it slows down his money" I said to her. She took the glass, tilted it on its side and we both watched as the beer slowly spilled out onto the ground. I knew Big Fred would've had a heart attack if he'd seen it. Everything was always about making money. "Do I have to choose?" I continued. I looked back at that stupid band on my finger and wanted so much just to take it off, stomp on it, and then feed it to the next dog that came my way.

"I've been wondering how long you were going to continue to let those men play you," she said.

"What can I say, Misty? I was in love with a man who has never known how to love—or even tried to read the book on it, just to get an idea."

"So you think it's all him, huh?"

"No, I know I went into this marriage with images of him as my knight that came to rescue the 'bright light' as he calls me."

"No, you don't get it." Misty raised her hand to her mouth; a cough had gotten stuck in her throat.

"I told you to take something for that cough of yours." I said to her in a joking but please take care of yourself, kind of way. She didn't respond to that but continued with the prior conversation.

"Okay, I'm going to tell you something that I know I should have told you a long time ago and for that I ask forgiveness. But just know that when I'm done, when I've told you, that you were partly to blame for my silence."

"What do you mean by that?" You could hear the fear in my voice.

"Well, ever since you married that man, you thought you were better than me. Tried to make me feel like you had achieved something more than I ever could."

"For a while, I hated you. But then I realized that if it were me and I came from where you came from and found a man that looked like that to marry me, well let's just say that I began to understand."

She was right. "I did get somewhat beyond myself there for a while, didn't I? I'm so sorry about that Misty. You have been the only person in my life that has been a friend to me."

Misty got a broad smile across her face. "Just remember those words when you make it big."

"Don't worry, I will—if that ever happens." I laughed. It provided somewhat of a calming sensation. "So what is it you were going to tell me?"

When she moved in closer and lowered her voice, it suddenly broke the lighthearted mood between us. I knew this would more than rock the ground I stood on; and I was right because I tell you, as I watched her lips move, I couldn't control my heart.

It's as if it were beating to its own rhythm; the rhythm of anxiety, the rhythm of me being torn apart, the rhythm of my emotions slowly breaking down, until there was not a speck of them left to be found.

But alas, when the story of "the meeting" was over, when her lips finally stopped moving, my emotions went from being lost to being slapped back into my body anew, and I was filled with a new emotion, one that I had never in my life felt before.

Even the ringing in my head had slowly begun to stop and rest for a moment. It had appeared that my emotions went on a train ride and when they returned, I picked up the color of vengeance.

If you have ever had a serious beating-up at school to the point that all you could think about was learning every possible way to fight back, you would know and you would understand a fraction of how I felt.

◯◉◯

# Chapter 12

"I looked at my man, my husband and said… 'Here's a little love for you' as I slid the back of my hand ever so neatly across his face. It was downright perfect."

**○◉○**

# Here's A Little Love for You

I remember walking back into that place filled with the essence of pure rage and seeing that man still slouched in that corner pushed up against some little thing of a woman and thinking how quickly a broken heart can change you.

Now don't get me wrong, reality was still a factor. What I mean, is that you don't just stop loving someone when you've given them the best part of you—your heartbeat. It's just that love, heartbeats and all, is easily overshadowed when rage is involved. You see, rage is beyond the capacity of anger. If anger is a piece of cold pie, rage is heating the pie up so that it tastes like something.

And as I stood in front of him, I heard the 'ding' of the microwave. This pie was done.

I saw the little thing look at me and then move quickly when she saw my hand slide into the upright position. I looked at my man, my husband, and said . . . "Here's a little love for you," as I slid the front of my hand ever so neatly across his face. It was downright perfect.

When I turned to walk away, I saw the little fat, bald man running up to me, a concerned look on this face. But I knew Big Fred was in on it. I knew it was all a fake. And I knew the evil root behind his fakeness. So before he could open his mouth, before he could spew the nonsense from his lips, I looked at him as squarely as I could in the darkness of The Skinny and said, "Glad I wasn't stupid enough to sign an exclusive agreement with you. I think this heart of mine is closed for business at The Skinny." I wanted him to know that I knew. As I walked out the front door, I felt another color being added to my box.

I heard footsteps rushing behind me, and I admit, I was afraid to turn around. I was afraid it would be him, Charles that is, trying to offer me some sad love song. I was afraid I would hear the lyrics again, write them in my heart, publish them in my mind, and then sign on the dotted line. How thankful I was to hear Misty's voice calling after me.

"Jazzmyne, slow down!"

I stopped and waited for her. I didn't care if she saw tears in my eyes. "Misty, please call me Naya, just like you did when I first walked into those doors because that's how I want to leave."

"Look, girl," Misty said, catching up. "You can't go changing your stage name. Too many people know you by that name now. But when it's just you and I, then I'll call you Naya."

All I could do was hug her. You know, it was the first time I had hugged someone who really didn't care what color was Jazzmyne.

"Misty, what I am going to do now?"

"I'll tell you what you're going to do, you're going to go home and call my brother. He's a real estate attorney for some rich couple that owns most of the property in New York."

"What is a real estate attorney going to do for me?"

"Well, he's got lots of friends—friends that handle divorces—and he will take good care of you and make sure that whatever attorney he gets to handle your case takes care of you."

"I don't have enough money for a divorce attorney, and I don't know anything about getting a divorce."

"Don't worry; my brother loves you. He's seen almost all your shows for the past year, only I never introduced you because it wasn't proper, you being married and all. When I say that he will take care of you, though, I mean just that!"

"I don't know, Misty."

"Look, he will do it, because I told him to. And you will do it, because you owe it to yourself not to be married to that man one second longer than you need to be. I mean it when I say that you don't have to worry about money; the divorce attorney will get it from Charles in the end. Trust me."

"Where do I stay?"

Misty shook her head. "Girl, you really don't know a thing, do you? Go home and call a locksmith to come and change the locks. Pack his bags and leave them outside the front door."

"Now, listen to me carefully. Don't you leave, because that could be called abandonment. You want the law to work in your favor, so he has to be the one to go—you're just going to help him with the process. Just remember that he was the one who went outside the marriage, so he'll have to pay you alimony."

"Yes, but don't I have to be able to prove that?"

"Girl, I've been waiting for you to get out of the clouds ever since he put that plastic ring on your finger. I've had my brother shooting pictures of him every time he walked out that door and it wasn't you on his arm. Trust me when I say that we have all the evidence you will need."

I didn't know what to say. I didn't even know how to say thank you—or anything else for that matter. All I could do was stand there and let the tears continue on their usual path. They always knew the way home, it seemed.

Then something dawned on me. "I wish there was some way to get back at Big Fred, Misty. It sounds like it was his idea that got the whole thing started. I bet if we thought about it, we could come up with something."

She stood silent and her look became serious, almost ashamed.

"What's wrong?" I said. "Why the silence?" Still she didn't answer, and that made me so nervous, I started to think that there was more she wasn't telling me. You know that saying "Be careful about thinking?" I obviously wasn't.

"Misty, I can't take it any longer. What aren't you telling me?"

"Look Naya, I can't help you get back at Big Fred."

"Why? You know what he did to me. Surely you can think of something."

"No, I'm sure I could and probably with very little effort, but . . . I can't, because, Naya . . . Big Fred is my father."

All I could do was turn and walk away. Reality had come back with a twist of "gotcha." Sure, I heard her calling after me, but I didn't turn around. I couldn't. I couldn't let her see me cry again. My life had been filled with nothing but tears, broken hearts, and crushed fantasies, caused by continually thinking that, finally, someone in this corrupt world really cared for me! I couldn't let her know that, she too, had me duped.

So it was at that exact moment when I followed the path I had taken so many years before, when I had dropped the last name Creek—when that beast, that thing, put his hands on me. It was at this particular point in time when I dropped the name Naya Moná. The world, it seemed, only wanted to color me Jazzmyne and I, for my part, was prepared to give them all an opportunity to take notice of each and every color that made up me.

I went home, called the locksmith, and packed Charles' things. Then I sat on something that was once considered a sofa and dared one tear to fall.

○ ◉ ○

# Chapter 13

"It seemed the darkness had come and removed two important colors from my box—the color of stupidity and the color of foolishness—and replaced them with one dramatic hue called growing up."

○ ◉ ○

# Growing Up

When the morning came and I looked into the mirror, I no longer saw a young, dumb twenty-year-old girl staring back. It seemed the darkness had come and removed two important colors from my box—the color of stupidity and the color of foolishness—and replaced them with one dramatic hue called growing up.

I was sure that, given time, those two old colors would find their way back into the mix of my other colors. In fact, I was positive it would happen. Actually, more than positive; I knew that the sureness of the matter was down-right realistic. Finally, I had decided to give into the possibilities of that big lesson that life had been trying to drive into me; that lesson about reality.

When I picked up the receiver to make the call that would end my marriage, I thought I wouldn't be able to find the right words. How do you say "I want a divorce," even to the man you're not divorcing? Turned out, the answer was not only simple, but rather poetic and amazingly non-complex: You make your words breathe.

How do you make words breathe? You start by opening your mouth, digging deep and speaking your mind. I spoke, he listened.

Once again, I found that freedom had been waiting for me just on the other side of the door and that all I had to do was open it and walk out. That's when I heard the knock upon my apartment door and realized that sometimes freedom comes at too high of a price. What I was about to learn made me realize that, if given the option, it would have been better to just declare bankruptcy.

There on the other side of the door stood Misty. Her face was covered in disbelief. Her makeup had been smeared by the millions of tears that had evidently fallen not too long ago. Her hands shook when our eyes made contact, and for a second I thought that I would have to reach out and catch her. This was the picture of reality, the color in my box that I had wanted to leave in the past with Naya Moná.

She didn't beat around the bush, as they say, didn't hold anything back, but leaned her weak body against my door post and opened her lips just wide enough to allow the words "Charles was killed last night when someone tried to rob him" slipped out.

My mind heard, my body reacted, and my heart went numb. It was her turn to get ready to catch me. It seemed my friend; the darkness had decided to visit me once again.

When my eyes opened, I was laying on the floor, holding my heart. The sadness made me want to say....How do I cry for you? How do I wipe the tears away that once longed to see even the specks of your face? How do I cry for you when every day I dreamt of loving you? How does my soul mix with yours now that your colors no longer exist? The last time we spoke, the last time we kissed, we were one. Now, I want to scream—wake up from that deep sleep my love. But I know your heart can't hear the lyrics that I send. How do I cry for you, my friend?

It's ironic, but there comes a point when the death of someone and love of someone sometimes feels the same. My heart broke because I loved him and my heart broke because I lost him.

The funeral came with so many mixed emotions. I'd watched people whom I have never seen, cry over the grave of my husband. When they began to speak of him, I swear there were moments when I wondered who they were talking about. In fact, one of those times, I looked in his coffin just to make sure I was at the right funeral. And I remember thinking, as some described him, that I would have loved to love such a man.

Not two weeks after the funeral, the landlord was banging on my door for the rent. I'd just started a small singing gig that Misty landed for me at a club called The Jazz Cat, and it was just enough to pay the rent and leave a few dollars in my pocket for food.

I admit, it was difficult for my heart to reclaim my friendship with Misty, but she had been there and stayed there for me after all was said and done, and the hatred that I had built over my wall of love had begun to melt away.

It's was a Tuesday afternoon and the rain was coming down like it had forgotten it paid a visit a few days back. There was a knock on my door and I'm not going to lie, I had been afraid to answer it. I figured it was either the landlord or something worse. Either way I figured it for bad news.

You know it seemed like ten years had flown by in the time it took for me to get from my bed, or should I say mattress to the front door.

"Are you Naya?"

I wasn't sure if I wanted to answer the man that stood in my doorway demanding a response. I kept looking at his suit and his well-polished shoes, thinking that both probably cost more than my rent for six months.

Now, some people might look at a man like that and think, *One day, I'm going to get a suit like that.* I didn't. You may find that hard to believe as you look around the place I live in today. But, you want to know what I thought? There were two things, actually.

First, I thought, *One day, my voice is going to be as polished as his shoes.* Second, I thought, *Charles once moved my heart in shoes like that.*

I did finally respond to the man once I found that I could stop looking at his well-polished, black leather shoes. "Yes, I am."

He reached out his hand and quickly produced a small business card. "Come to this address tomorrow at 10:00 with your attorney. Please be on time."

When he left, I picked up the phone, dialed Misty's brother and began to breathe.

○ ◉ ○

# Chapter 14

"Little did I know that those perfectly polished black
leather shoes of his had been worth ten times more than
the ring he put on my finger."

○ ◉ ○

# Perfectly Polished

The morning came with its own anxieties, as I walked into a plush conference room and sat in plush seats and drank what I'm sure was plush water, if there is such a thing. Misty's brother had fixed me up with some attorney that I had never seen, had barely spoken to—except for once on the phone, just the night before—and was sure, would not show up.

The conversation that proceeded as he walked in and everyone sat in their plush seats taught me two important lessons. One: when money is involved, always have an attorney. And two: to some attorneys, you are worth nothing more than a dollar sign. In fact, I could count on one hand how many times my actual name was used. More often, I was simply referred to as "her," "the wife," or "my client."

Well, it turned out that my husband, my Charles, was not just some investor. When the attorneys began to talk about what they termed "his worth," I gulped my water a million times just to keep myself from standing up and screaming.

You see, Charles had led me to believe that he had very little financially but could more than make up for that in his love for me. What can I say about that, but what I already have? I was young, dumb, and in love with his polished leather shoes. Little did I know that those perfectly polished black leather shoes of his had been worth ten times more than the ring he put on my finger.

That man had me living in a tiny one-bedroom apartment, sleeping on a raggedy old mattress because he said we couldn't afford a bed, and watching every dime I made for "us" at The Skinny. And all the while, he was taking his "little things" to his upstate five-bedroom penthouse! Screaming would have been an understatement. I wanted to take his money and charge him interest for all the tears I had shed over him!

That afternoon, I walked out of that conference room with three things. First was my pride, which I was clutching in one hand; second was my heart, which I was holding in the other. Somehow, when the meeting was all over, they'd both tried to pack up and leave me. The third thing I walked out with was a check for twenty thousand dollars. The rest of Charles T. Williams' worth went to pay off all the investment loans he had taken out. Even his precious penthouse, the one that I had never seen, would have to be sold to pay them off.

Speaking of which, I had requested only one small thing of his all morning—namely, the keys to his penthouse.

Not so that I could go and imagine what it would have been like to live there. No, I wanted to go and get those perfectly polished black leather shoes of his. I wanted to keep them so that I remember what I saw the first time I looked down at them—then every time my heart tried to reach those feelings again, I could slap myself back into reality rather than live in what never became one.

Now, I know you're probably wondering what was the first thing that I did with that money. Well, I called Misty up, and she and I went out and purchased me a brand new bed, a brand new mattress, and a real sofa. Then I called my landlord, demanded a new apartment, and Misty and I went and had ourselves a steak. It was my first one.

For the next six months, I sang my lungs out at The Jazz Cat until I got a call from Misty.

"Hey, Jazzmyne, do you remember that man you told me that you met at The Skinny that night?

"What man?"

"The one that wanted you to come and sing in his live band, and you told him no."

"You mean, Mr. Cooper." I had known the whole time but wanted to give her a hard time since she'd seemed so excited.

"Yeah, he's the one I'm talking about."

"Okay," I said. "You've refreshed my memory. Now, why is going down memory lane so important?"

"Well, he came in the other night looking for you. Said that he wanted to speak with you but that he wasn't getting anywhere trying to reach you at The Jazz Cat. They kept telling him to go speak with your manager."

"What manager? I don't have a manager."

"Sure you do."

"Who?"

"Me."

"You told him you were my manager?"

"No, I told him I was your friend and the closest thing you had to a manager."

"I see. What did he say?"

"Well, he said that he wants you to come and audition for him, because they are ready to cut an album but still need a voice to make it complete."

"What voice?"

"*Your* voice, of course. Girl, don't act like you don't know you can blow."

"Well, I guess I need to get a manager." There was a pause on the other end. I knew that idea probably made her nervous, so I laughed to break the tension. "Okay, since you're my manager, when do we go see him?"

"Jazzmyne, thank you. But I want you to know that you don't have to make me your manager. I will still be there for you no matter what."

"I know that, but I don't want you just to be there for me; I want you to be there *with* me."

"Jazzmyne, I have got to tell you something that I know you don't want to hear or even want to talk about. But before we get into this together, I need to clear my mind. That night when I told you that Big Fred was my father, you walked away from me before I could explain."

"You see, I started working for my father when I was seventeen, just like you, and I saw many singers come and go and leave him with nothing. Every one of them moved on to become something and never gave him credit for the start he gave them. Not one."

"I know what he was trying to do to you was dead wrong, but I also know that he did it because he thought you were his ticket to the fame pie that he never got a slice of. None of that had anything to do with why I didn't tell you about his scheme with Charles. What I did tell you was the truth, every bit of it. I just want you to know that, I need you to understand that."

"Look, Misty, none of that matters to me anymore."

"I realize that, but it matters to me. I only work for my father so that one day I can open my own jazz club. It has always been my dream. He is my father in name only, as far as I am concerned."

It was the first time I heard her cry, and it made me feel stupid for letting that moment back at The Skinny go on for as long as I did.

"You're my friend Misty, but tomorrow when we go in to see Mr. Copper, I don't need a friend. I need a manager and an attorney."

"Well then, let me get off this phone and call my brother."

"Misty?'

"Yeah?"

"Thank you."

And with the click of the receiver, another color was added to my box.

○ ◎ ○

# Chapter 15

"Well, when I step out onto that stage, Mr. Wesley, I put
my foot in my voice and give it all the love I can."

## You Think You Can Sing

It was the first morning in a long time that I woke up with a smile on my face, not to mention an outlook on my dreams that reflected nothing but sunshine. It was the morning of my audition, and I felt I was born to sing. I realized that my voice was my talent in life, and it was at that point that the art of singing, the thrill of hearing music breathe life into my tired, rusty old bones, became my passion.

Misty and I and another attorney that Misty's brother had found for me, showed up at the audition, but we hadn't expected to see the long line of women waiting to do exactly what I was hoping to do: get my voice on an album. Looking at all of them, knowing only one of us would be selected, made my nerves want to start running toward the bus station. I could already hear my lungs beginning to crack and the air in them drying up to almost nothing.

"Don't worry, girl, he wants you. The rest of these girls are just for show." Misty slid right into the manager role, saying just the thing my bones needed to hear to make me sit up straight.

The attorney's name was Clint Wesley and he specialized in entertainment law. He sat opposite from me on his phone, but I knew he had one eye on me. I wondered *what* he even knew about me. I must have had my questions stamped on my forehead, because once he was off his phone, he walked over to me, sat down, and opened his briefcase. From it, he produced a slim yellow folder that had a single picture of me on the front of it, and a piece of paper covered in handwriting on the inside.

"So you think you can sing?" he asked me.

"I wouldn't be sitting out here if I didn't, now would I?" I responded.

"What makes you think you can sing better than them?" He pointed to the line of women who looked much older than I was.

I smiled at him, eager to answer. "I'm sure even a big-shot entertainment attorney remembers his mama cooking him his favorite dish, don't you?"

"Sure, but what does that have to do with my question?"

"Why was that dish that your mama made so good to you and probably to everyone else that came over to your house? I'll answer the question for you: because every time she made that dish, she did as the saying goes and 'put her foot in it.' She gave it all the love she could. Well, when I step out onto that stage, Mr. Wesley, I put my foot in my voice and give it all the love I can."

Mr. Wesley grabbed a pen out of his briefcase and began scribbling.

I looked at what he was writing. "Why did you write down what I just said?"

"Because when we get in there, your voice might get you on the stage, but it's how I present you on the floor that sells you. Everyone must have a pitch, Ms. Jazzmyne, and it can't be the same as everyone else's. It has to be something different, something that makes them see that you're the only woman for the part. And who else knows why you're the best, better than yourself?"

I looked at Misty and saw her trying to hide the smile that was forming ever so slightly upon her face. What can I say? He had me.

Then after putting the yellow folder back in his brief-case and setting it down on the ground next to him, he turned and looked me in the eye.

"Your real name is Naya Moná Creek," he said softly, so that only I could hear him. "Born in Chicago, Illinois, to Jonathan Kenneth Creek—who, by the way, had a Missing Children report put out on you when you ran away from home at the age of seventeen."

"You started your singing career at a small but rather well-known place called The Skinny. You married Charles T. Williams, a real estate investor when you were eighteen. After almost two years of his going outside the marriage, you began divorce proceedings, only Mr. Williams was killed when someone tried to rob him."

"He left you nothing but debt, although when it was all said and done, you were able to walk away with a check for twenty thousand dollars. You changed your address but only to a different apartment number in the same building. I assume you did this to give yourself a fresh start. You are now working at a jazz club called The Jazz Cat and it can barely pay your rent. Don't worry Jazzmyne, I know who you are. It's what I get paid to do."

Before I could open my mouth to catch my breath and deliver some type of response, I heard my name being called.

"Jazzmyne," Mr. Copper said as I stood. "I'm so glad you were able to make it. Your manager said she'd get you here one way or the other. I'm glad it was alive and ready to sing."

I tried to issue a small laugh at his half-joke, while focusing on restraining myself, in particular, keeping my hand from flying across the face of Mr. Wesley.

"Please give your resume to Mrs. Collins before going up on stage," said Mr. Copper, "and then we'll give you a few minutes to warm up with the band before your audition."

How do you describe panic? All you had to do was look at my face to get the definition. I turned to Misty and saw her reach into the large bag that was draped on her right shoulder. She pulled out an envelope and handed it to the lady who I assumed was Mrs. Collins. She then gave me a sly, on-the-side sort of wink and ushered me toward the stage. This was the moment when my talent became my passion, and my passion became my talent. After this moment, I would never again separate the two.

I remember stepping onto that stage and looking out past Mr. Wesley, past Misty, and even past Mr. Copper, who sat with a big grin on his face. I focused on the empty seat just in the corner of my right eye. Then I parted my lips and allowed the music to enter, seeping deep into my veins, flowing past my kidneys, pumping slowly into my lungs. And when it hit just the tip of my heart, I heard my mind saying, *There now, girl. Take it slow, because you're finally here.*

Then letting out the sigh of inner peace, I felt the air inside me begin to return. My thoughts began to skip to the beat, and every other part of me joined in on the melody. I was more than in tune; I was floating ever so softly, ever so gently, right into the heart of possibility.

I had barely opened my eyes, ready to return to the land of the audition, when I felt the presence of Mr. Wesley right in front of the stage, staring at me. "You know, I think that was way better than my mother's spaghetti and meatball dinner. In fact, I'd say you put more than one foot in that song. I'd say you put your life into those lyrics."

I wanted so much to enjoy that moment, but having gotten to know reality so well over the past few months— good to you one moment and slapping you the next—I didn't. My skin was getting thick to the point that I hoped to one day respond to a statement like Mr. Wesley's with "Is that all you got?"

I had thought about just getting down off the stage and walking past him, but that thought must have abandoned ship, because I stepped off the stage, deliberately placing one foot in front of the other, to ensure that he noticed.

I kept my head down, so I could focus on his shoes and allow myself to feed off of the performance high that was still in me. Then, when the moment was tender and ripe, I looked up, straight into the tiny cracks of his face, and said, "My voice is what will pay for your next pair of perfectly polished black leather shoes." With that, I walked away just as slowly as I had gotten off that stage. It was all that needed to be said.

"Jazzmyne," Mr. Cooper said as he approached me, laughing. "That was amazing! In fact, it was better than I bragged it would be. I think you sang better today than when I first heard and approached you a while back. The decision, of course, is not mine, but I know they heard what I heard."

I saw him turn to look at the "they" he referred to, and so I raised my voice just loud enough so that "they" could hear me. "Mr. Copper, I am sure that since the band and the album, if not already, will be named after you, there should be no question as to who will be the female on the cover once it is released. Now, my manager and my attorney are here to carry out the fine print of the matter, but the decision in your head is already final. Don't you agree?"

I turned to Misty and Mr. Wesley and said in the same tone, "Either they make the decision now to match what's in his head, or I walk out that door."

I stepped back and looked at everyone, waiting for what seemed an eternity but for what was literally more like a minute. Mr. Copper walked over to Misty and Mr. Wesley and said, "Where do we sign for her?" My gut had told me he was really the one.

You see, I have learned that people have a certain way they want to color you, so you must be the one to decide which color it will be.

For the next six months, I sang nights at The Jazz Cat, but banging it out in the daytime in the studio with Mr. Copper.

# Chapter 16

"I'm talking about controlling your colors: owning your box and then only pulling out of it, the color you deem necessary for each situation."

**○ ⊙ ○**

# Controlling My Colors

D o you know how liberating it is to walk in your own space? I'm not talking about your own actual living space, although that can be just as liberating. No, I'm talking about being in your own space in a way that you alone determine the colors in your box at any given moment in your life—no, let me back up—at any given second in your life. It's like going down that expensive street in New York and knowing that everything in those stores you can afford but only if you want to. I'm talking about controlling your colors: owning your box and then only pulling out of it, the color you deem necessary for each situation.

That day at the audition, was the moment in my life when I finally began to take control of my box. I allowed myself to be the one to select the next color that popped out. I looked at the situation at hand and reached in, grabbed the color Jazzmyne and colored myself in it. What was the situation? Don't worry I'm about to tell you.

Before I go there, I should tell you that answering—*how* you get to such a moment in your life, is not the pertinent question that demands a response. No, the question that demands a response—the one that I'm about to answer for you is: *Why*.

It started the day the album release came upon me like a whirlwind, almost knocking me off my feet and causing me to lose my balance, my color. I was just soaking my feet in that emotion when my phone rang.

"Jazzmyne, its Chris Wesley," said the voice on the other end.

Not even a hello fell off my lips. With him, I had found it was the only way to maintain my color.

"I have to ask you a really tough question," he said.

"What is it?"

"How well do you know Misty?"

"Enough to call her my closet friend."

"Jazzmyne, in this business, you will learn to never have friends. That day at the auditions, when Misty handed that woman what I thought was your resume, it turned out to be an exclusive management agreement.

"The agreement stated that, as your manager, Misty would get sixty percent of all royalties and the like earned by you, her client, for a period of no less than five years. Now you know that my firm's representation fee is twenty percent, so you do the math on your take."

"I have been going back and forth with Mr. Copper's attorneys on the agreement that I presented on behalf of you as our client, which indicated that she was only entitled to twenty percent of any royalties and the like for a period of no more than three years but no less than one."

"The problem is that your signature on our agreement—the one that I had drawn up—exactly matches your signature on the agreement that Misty presented. Since the contract she presented was dated prior to mine, a Judge, if we took this to court, could rule that hers is binding. What do you want to do?"

I was sitting on my newly purchased couch, holding the phone in my right hand, because my left hand was too busy wiping my tear-stained cheeks. I kept telling myself to get it together, to not let this man hear me lose my color, but my emotions didn't seem to be listening to the words of wisdom my mind was whispering to them. In fact, in one particular moment, I couldn't even breathe. Thank goodness a moment is only temporary.

"Jazzmyne, are you there?" said Mr. Wesley.

"Yes."

"What do you want to do?"

"Get control."

"Okay, I'll see if I can pull a few strings and speak privately to a Judge, and then we'll take it from there."

"Okay."

"I'll call you tomorrow."

Again, I didn't respond, but this time for an entirely different reason. It was all I could do to hang up the phone and get going. I needed to run and catch my heart, which had come up and out of my throat, escaped to the train station, and gotten a one-way ticket to a place called, No Return.

**○ ◎ ○**

# Chapter 17

"I felt like saying to everyone who wanted to color me
their own way, 'This voice is closed for business.'"

## This Voice Is Closed for Business

It took a whole week for Mr. Wesley to get back in touch with me. But to be fair, it took a whole week for me to get back in touch with me. My emotions seemed to have completely shut down. I found myself throwing things and screaming every night. It was more than tough. It was the realization that this was my nightmare to handle, to get control of and I, at that moment, couldn't.

Everyone in my life thus far had tried to deceive me in some fashion; with all the used crayons in my life thus far, I was sure my box had to be running empty. I mean how much coloring could a woman take! It was an answer I was terrified even to acknowledge, let alone embrace. I felt like saying to everyone who wanted to color me their own way, "This voice is closed for business."

Colors are a beautiful thing when *you* can determine their make-up, their essence, the way they appear in you—layered and mixed with your other hues. But flip the script, as they say—leave your box open too long and your crayons free for the taking—and colors assume an essence that can ruin your very core. Left in others hands, colors either leave a scribbled-up mess in you or they dry up completely, having gone unused. Either way, you're left with just a shadow of what you used to be—without your real color and without your real name.

Then there was banging on my front door. I had heard someone knocking before, but my mind had not cared to answer it. Now, it seemed, that they were getting impatient with me. I didn't really care about that either. My feet dragged and I felt my hand reach out and touch the coldness of the brass knob.

In the doorway stood Mr. Copper, with a fake "How have you been, where have you been and we've missed you" sort of smile on his face. You see, I had figured out that if

Misty gave him one contract and Mr. Wesley gave him another, he should've said something.

I decided rather quickly not to play games with him. "I see you and Misty took a ride together with my life in the back seat."

That smile he had disappeared, but was fast replaced with a look of "So you found out—who cares?" Out loud though, all he said was, "Look, five years is nothing in this business. You're young, and frankly, no one makes money in this business on their first deal. You always get the short end; it's just how the game is played. Don't take what's business, personal. I learned that many years ago. And it's not my fault that you let personal and business mix." He smiled and continued.

"Anyway, we need to see you at the studio tomorrow. Read your contract if you get any other ideas and decide to take off. It clearly states that you're obligated to be there, every day or we start docking your pay. Remember also, you don't make much off this thing as it is; I'd hate to see you working for free."

I wanted to slam the door or throw something at him, but I did neither. Instead, I smiled and showed every single tooth in my mouth. Then I walked up to him and spoke, without a flutter in my voice and without stumbling over one single syllable.

"Know that I will be there tomorrow and I will sing. But what comes out of these lungs of mine . . . who knows? In fact, I think I'm coming down with a five-year cold. So, if you want something else to come out, then I suggest you talk to Misty, and then you and she get in the back seat and put my life back up front where it belongs!"

Ten minutes after I closed the door gently after him, my phone rang. I knew it was Misty, so I didn't bother to answer. Got to get this control, I mean this color, away from her and back in my box, fresh and ready before I decide to have *that* conversation with her.

It took another week, but finally I was ready to do what I needed to do: dig deep and speak my mind. Remember, there is a deliberate process to letting your words breathe. This time, I had decided to let mine glide through the air and rest upon the clouds, before coming back down with lightning and thunder. It went a little something like this.

First, the gliding-through-the-air part. There were many steps I needed to take for that one. One involved calling an attorney that I'd found in the phone book who offered free consultations. I wanted to know the rules on hiring minors in a club, find out whether there were laws allowing them to serve drinks beyond the punch level.

Why? Well, remember I told you that I'd started working at The Skinny when I was just seventeen. And, in fact, I started serving drinks on day one. Equipped with that information, I felt like I was refueling, like the color was coming back into my cheekbones, filling me with just a hint of attitude—and that, my friend, can be a beautiful color.

Second, I had finally figured out how they got my signature on that agreement that Mr. Copper received. It was simple, really. About two months after I had started working for Big Fred, Misty came into the back room and told me I needed to sign an employment application. I was so busy, and as always, the place was dark and foggy. So I put my signature on the form without even reading it. It would be a mistake I would never repeat.

Now loaded with all the facts and an approach, I was eager to play their game. But, before I had a chance to even deal the cards, Mr. Wesley called. The phone literally rang as I was about to pick up the receiver and dial the digits that would send my voice to the clouds, where they would have surely reverberated and returned like thunder.

"Jazzmyne," Mr. Wesley said. "I need to ask you a question that could play a big role in how this thing turns out."

It was beginning to be a normal thing between Mr. Wesley and I, the formality of our calls. There was no "Hello" or "How have things been?" No, it was more like "This is what it is" or "This is how it needs to be." Pure business.

"Go ahead," I said curtly. He didn't take offense.

"Do you remember signing anything at The Skinny prior to your eighteenth birthday?"

"I signed what I thought was an employment application—but I have determined since then that it must have been this mysterious agreement that Misty gave to Mr. Copper."

"Are you sure?"

"Yes, I'm sure. Why?"

"Well, the law states that minors can't sign legal agreements without the consent of a parent or legal guardian. Was your father present?"

"Do I really need to answer that?"

"For the record, yes you do."

"No, my father was not present."

"And you're sure there was no way they could have gotten written consent from him prior?"

"I'm positive."

"Perfect, that makes the agreement not binding in a court of law. So how do you want to handle this?"

"You're my attorney, so call Misty and fire her."

"I will have to go before the Judge and present the new facts so he can sign off. But after that, I will call her and take care of the matter. Jazzmyne, for the record, please don't sign anything without reading it first—and even then, don't sign it until I've had a chance to look at it."

"Okay, I said. "But let me ask you something now. How well do you know Misty's brother?"

"I don't really know him. Actually, I've never even seen him before. He works on the real estate side of my firm. We have a lot of attorneys on that side of the firm, but only a few that handle entertainment law. I was given the choice to take your case or not."

"So why did you take it?"

"Because your father is Jonathan Kenneth Creek, and my firm is owned by Kenneth and Sarah Creek. I told you I knew who you were."

There went my color again.

# PART THREE

○ ◉ ○

# Chapter 18

"Why is it that it becomes so important for us to know where we come from, the moment we realize that we have roots? It's like the not knowing causes a burning inside of us that only knowledge and facts can put out."

○ ⊙ ○

# Finding Your Roots

I have often wondered what I'd see if I looked up the word *roots* in the dictionary. Would they use my life as an example of the definition? Something like, "Here are the roots that colored Jazzmyne."

Why is it that it becomes so important for us to know where we come from, the moment we realize that we have roots? It's like the not knowing causes a burning inside of us that only knowledge and facts can put out; which is why this moment felt like a flame.

I need to stop now, take a deep pause and direct my attention and words back to my son for just a moment. It has been a while, but he's still here, listening to a "Once upon a time" story. However, there was something in this burning moment that reminded me of him. There was something more I needed to explain to him about roots, a wisdom that I wanted to share.

I said to him, "You spoke about pieces of a puzzle and not having them all or not being able to make them all fit together. But the metaphor I give you is much more, because what you're really talking about is finding your roots. Your roots help make up the colors in your crayon box. Don't think for a moment that you don't have one too—your own crayon box. We all have colors.

"You see; when I talk about colors, understand that what I mean is that colors can be journeys, attitudes, emotions, or even moments. Colors can refer to the color of your skin or what someone tries to make you. But roots are something very different, because roots are the insides of the people that gave you your colors—your ancestors. So when you understand your roots, you automatically understand some of your colors." I wasn't finished.

"You roared about giving your children your history, but I whisper this question: what is history? History is nothing more than the actions that people before you took in the journeys of their lives.

"Since we've met, I've given you my colors, but I've also given you my roots. I've shown you what's inside me. You might say that I've charted my DNA out for you, shown you the stuff I'm made of. Roots are like the very essence of something deep, something beyond skin. They are the stuff that makes your heart tick to its own rhythm." I was reaching the climax of my point now.

"The beast, the man you thought was the person you could call Daddy—his roots began with what his mother was made of. The nasty flavors inside that woman gave him his color."

I was ready to dive into this moment in my life, when I noticed the clock on the wall. The time seemed to be staring at me, commanding my attention. So I gave in. It was time to bring this moment to an end—at least for now.

Watching him leave was not as emotional as the first time. In fact, I was more exhausted than anything else. I felt like a pot. And the story I'd just told was like water inside of me. It became heated and then began to boil. And then it boiled over, making a big mess all over the place.

The mess of my life just boiled out of me. Thankfully, though, there will be a time when I come to my senses, turn down the flame, and clean up the mess; but not today. I hadn't gotten that far in the story yet. We still had a lot more boiling over to do.

Climbing into my bed and staring at the ceiling, I began to think about the many pictures of my son's children that I had seen over time. They looked so much like him. Two little girls with brown curly hair, hazel brown eyes, and smiles that would make me go broke. I'd like to think that the eye color came from me, but I didn't have any pictures of their mother. What was she like? You know, pictures give you only so much to imagine, very little room for "fill in the blank," and almost nothing to color in the missing spots.

I wondered what it was like when he asked her to marry him despite his past. Did he expect her to love him past the pain of not knowing? Love can sometimes put out even the hottest flame, but in the end, our past always seems to flare up out of nowhere.

I wondered what she thought about him coming to see me. Did she tell him he didn't need me in his life since he had her? I'd like to think that she tried to encourage him to see me with an open mind. Or did she prepare him for the possibility that maybe I wouldn't have one, an open mind, that is. Perhaps, she told him that I wouldn't want to let all the tiny details of my life just boil over? Whatever she said, I knew that she had to be a strong woman, because he was a strong man. He would have to be; he had my roots and even inherited some of my colors.

As I drifted off to sleep, I thought, *tomorrow I will add another color to his box.* Time to flip the script.

**O ⊙ O**

# Chapter 19

"It was a position that said he was ready for whatever I gave him, and so I decided to put it to the test. I decided to see just how strong he really was."

○ ◉ ○

# Confident Position

Another day, another pot added to the stove. But that was okay. I was ready for him to come, sit, and just watch the water boil. In fact, I was already sitting in my office when he walked in.

It was strange, but he seemed to be in a good mood. I think I even saw him smile as he sat and crossed his legs in a rather confident position. It was a position that said he was ready for whatever I gave him, and so I decided to put it to the test. I decided to see just how strong he really was.

I walked around the desk and positioned myself on the sofa next to the chair he was sitting in. I placed my left hand on top of the right, so that he would see the ring on my left finger. He did. Maybe he'd think I was holding onto the memories of a dead and loveless husband. I would let that color float around in his crayon box and get all mixed up with the others, but just for a moment.

I waited until we made eye contact again, slowly positioning my focus so that when I decided to begin where I had left off the day before, I could watch his mannerisms, his posturing, his interest.

He was sitting on the edge of his seat. Perfect. I began my narration, with year two of my working with Mr. Copper.

That year flew in upon me, saying "hello" with a force that felt like someone was knocking me upside my head. Misty and I had barely spoken since I'd learned what she'd done, and as far as I was concerned, her color was no longer a part of my box. Mr. Wesley, whom I had begun to call Chris, lived up to his word and fired her one day after her year was up. Had to maintain the agreements in my contract, but I tell you I couldn't wait to walk into the studio and not see her face!

Now, you are probably wondering if she ever tried to explain herself. The answer is not really. She, Big Fred, and my late husband had created what they thought was a masterpiece of a scheme that, for the most part, involved them licking their fingers to count the green stuff and my singing like a fool to help them accomplish their dreams.

So when I laid out my past for her on a blanket, she simply wrapped herself in it and wore it like a coat; especially when I told her the name of my father. To her, the fact that her brother worked for my grandparents' firm was just too big of an opportunity to pass over.

Telling her my life's story had been a product of being young and dumb. Both of which, had almost cost me my sanity. To be honest, I had to fight the colors that existed every moment I had the thought of just reaching out and giving her a little touch of my skin. That would have been the Naya in me. The Jazzmyne in me, however, was at least strong enough by then to decide to color the moment deeper than a touch of skin. Remember, Big Fred had a passion for two things—music and money—so I decided to hit him hard on the money side.

I had him investigated for hiring minors and allowing them to sell liquor, and when the fines started pouring in, they couldn't afford to keep the place open. Anyway, when it was all said and done, let's just say that The Skinny would never again get fat off the hard work and misfortune of people like me. And that when all of it went down the way it did, I thought I had finally reached a moment in my life when I could allow myself to breathe instead of just my words.

But then, just as I was about to draw my first breath, another issue arose inside me. It was the issue of my grandparents, Kenneth and Sarah Creek. It had been some time since Chris had dropped the bomb on me, exploding my mind with the not-knowing-my-roots factor. When he had first told me, I had come to the conclusion that I didn't care to know. Why? I mean, I had lived with that beast for seventeen years and not once during that time had they ever spoken to me, visited me, or so much as sent me a card that recognized I existed.

And as much as I wished that I could have just left it at that, well, as I said before, the not knowing is a burning that can only be put out with the facts—and let's just say that by that point in my life, I was scorched, and that no other extinguisher but knowledge (trust me—I tried them all) had enough force to keep my longing to know at bay.

It was at this point in my story that I said to my son, "I guess I say all of that to say that I understand why you are here. I understand how the absence of roots can be a powerful intoxication." But then it was back to the main story.

The second album was scheduled to make its appearance on the music scene, but this time, the album was titled *Jazzmyne, Featuring The Coppers* instead of the other way around. The second album brought me a new contract, a new manager, much better pay, and the right to begin to take control of even more colors in my life.

They say that the album topped the jazz charts longer than any other album. Strange thing about that was the album told a lot about me. Well, it should have, I guess, since I'd written most of the songs. In fact, if I'd been given the choice, I would have called the album *Color Me Jazzmyne*. Anyway, I won several awards for that album, including all the big ones.

It was at this moment that I started writing songs for other artists. I found that the concept of song writing was where the real colors of control and money were at. It wasn't a passion but it began to pay more than the bills.

And believe it or not, The Coppers and I were still just performing at The Jazz Cat during that time, although very quickly it became obvious that I needed a bigger arena, so we started to tour.

My voice began to trail off for a moment. I needed to stop and come back to the present, needed to address my son directly. This part was too important.

"Life was like hot fudge melting just right on a piece of chocolate cake," I said to him. "Well, it would have been like that, had it not been for that roots thing, still burning up my insides. And then, on top of that, a second issue had begun to arise, keeping me up at night. Guess what that was… itwas you. . . ."

I knew that statement would change his position.

**⦿ ⊙ ⦿**

# Chapter 20

"Turn the other cheek and never give in to the need.
Look at those shoes, girl. Look at those perfectly polished
black leather shoes and remember reality."

**○ ◉ ○**

# Turn the Other Cheek

S uccess was coming at me like a wave, one after another. Peace, for me, however, was more like an ocean that was too deep, with waves so strong, it was as if peace could never find its way to me. Every night, my brain seemed to refuse to rest. It was like my thoughts would run off in the night in search of peace, only to return in the morning empty-handed. Lack of peace is a difficult emotion to tend with. It seems to always win.

And so, as I'd done several mornings during that time, I woke up with tears streaking my face. I wasn't sure how I would deal with the emotions that were flooding what had become a seemingly stable existence for me, so I went back

to the method that had carried me thus far: I dialed Chris'
phone number so I could let my words breathe. Why break
something that's already working?

As usual, he answered on the second ring. It was a fact
that he had been reminding me of lately—the fact that he
was always there. That he would always answer my call.

"I need to talk to you," I said.

"What time do you want me to come over?"

Chris didn't ask questions like, "Do you need me to
come over?" And he would never ask, "What is it about?"
Rather, he would just respond to me. His response was
becoming like a comfort food to me; however, it was that
thought that scared me. I found myself thinking, *don't let
him get too close. Don't open that place in your heart and
hand him the key. Close off that part of you that wants to feel
that emotion. Turn the other cheek and never give into the
need. Look at those shoes, girl. Look at those perfectly polished
black leather shoes and remember reality.* It was hard. I was
losing that color.

When I heard his knock at my door, I felt my heart
flutter and a slow smile slide across my face. When I

opened it, he stood in front of me with a "got here as fast as I could" kind of grin.

Chris was hitting somewhere around six feet, perhaps a little over. His eyes were like the ocean, and I always thought that I could easily find myself asking for a lifeguard if I got caught in them. When he smiled, even if it were dark in the room, you could see just as clearly as if the sun were shining in your face. He always wore a dark suit with a modern shirt and a spunky flavor of a tie. And, of course, there were the shoes. Clearly, I was losing that color of reality; lately, I seemed to lose it every time Chris set foot inside my door.

"When are you going to move out of this place?" That was his greeting to me that day. It was a question that stuck me rather oddly, because frankly I had never really given it much thought. The place was full of my colors; they were written on the walls and drawn upon the furniture.

"Find me a new one," I said, simply.

"How soon do you want to move?"

"Just let me know when to come and sign the paper-work."

He nodded.

Then I completely changed gears on him. "I need to find my son."

"How long has it been since you saw him?"

"Ten years."

"I see." He paused for a moment. "Do you know what he would look like today?"

"In my dreams, yes, but in reality, no."

"What's his name?"

"I don't know. I never got a chance to give him one."

"I take it his last name would have been Creek, am I right?"

It was a hard question to answer. Chris and I had never been down such a private road together. I wondered, *do I tell him what color is Jazzmyne?*

But before I could answer that question, he said, "It explains a lot."

"What do you mean?" I was puzzled and scared all at the same time.

"Why you married Charles."

"So you think you've got my colors all figured out?" I was going back into my shell. Putting up my defenses and closing my box. He knew it, but he didn't back down.

"You married Charles thinking he could give you what was taken away from you. What every child needs and deserves to have, a feeling of peace and security and the comfort of love."

How I hated that he knew me so well, so deep. It was like he was all up in my box. And now, I found myself begging the tears not to pay me a visit, downright pleading with them not to, but then I heard that doorbell again and I had to answer. There they were, my friends the tears, with bags this time, apparently ready to stay for a while. I had to turn my back to him. I wasn't ready for him to see that color in my box.

"Chris . . . " Even as I said his name, I could feel him behind me, and I knew that he had taken a step closer. I could feel his breath upon the back of my neck.

"I'll wait, Naya," he said, almost in a whisper. "But the day will come when your last name will change and your box will be filled with the colors you deserve."

I didn't turn around until I heard my front door open and shut. He had let me off the hook, and, I admit, I was thankful.

Probably twenty minutes passed when I heard another knock on my door. I opened the door and recognized the face almost instantly, though I hadn't seen it in quite some time. It was the divorce attorney. He wanted to set up another appointment with me at the law firm. They had to tell me, he said, though in not so many words, about some colors they had just recently discovered in my ex-husband.

I remember thinking, *do they want their money back? If so, I have at least that much in my wallet.*

○ ◉ ○

# Chapter 21

"I'm not blowing my own horn; I'm just saying
I didn't feel like, 'here we go again.'"

# Here We Go Again

O nce again, I found myself back in that plush conference room, sitting in those plush chairs, though sipping tea instead of water. However, this time I didn't feel uncomfortable. You see, I had a little bit of the plush thing going on myself. In fact, this time when I walked into that room, they didn't treat me, even address me, as just some client. No, it was more like, "Good morning Ms. Jazzmyne, the famous jazz singer." I'm not blowing my own horn; I'm just saying I didn't feel like "here we go again."

Chris was there, of course, and the other attorney who had originally delivered the bombshell to me years back. I didn't say a word. I didn't have to. It turned out that the first time they commanded I come here, they hadn't properly done their investigation of what they now referred to as Mr. Charles T. Williams' estate. And so this time, when I excused them from my presence, I walked out with everything intact: my heart, my pride and a check with more zeros in it than I care to share.

I also walked out with the knowledge that there was now a buyer interested his penthouse. And that buyer, and his wife, just happened to have the same last name as I did. Within seconds of the meeting ending, the plans had been arranged; I was to meet with them privately at my home office the following day. Finally, the hope for my burning to be quashed had come. I didn't sleep that night.

The next day, he walked into my office with an air of confidence that I had never seen; just the right amount of cockiness and an aroma of authority that left everyone in his presence sniffing the air, breathing it in. It was Mr. Kenneth Creek.

He was nothing like the beast. His speech was skilled and always to the point. He looked you in the eye and never backed down. Even his cologne seemed to command your attention. I didn't dare look at his shoes. I just sat at my desk trying to keep my knees quiet. I mean, how do you look at your roots in the eye and not ask why?

When he opened his mouth, all I could do was sit there and watch his lips move. I honestly can't remember the first words that came out of his mouth. Like I said before, roots can be intoxicating. But at one point at the beginning of our conversation, he said, "You look just like your mother."

"You should know," I said. "She was also your granddaughter."

"Sad, yes, but true. However, before you try to go down that road, let me just tell you that I won't."

The aroma in the air turned to a stink that made me want to open the window—not as much to air out the place, but rather, to jump. My longing to know was the only thing that kept me pinned to my seat.

"What can I do for you, Mr. Creek?" I said.

"You don't have to be so formal, Naya."

"I'm sorry, where are my manners. Was I supposed to stand up and welcome you with open arms?"

"That tone doesn't work for me."

"Really, please enlighten me by telling me what tone I should use." I'd tried to put as much attitude in that statement as I could muster.

"You have that same edge as Jonathan."

Okay, forget about me jumping out the window; at this point, I wanted him to go first. I looked at him firmly and said, "So that each of us understands the boundaries of this conversation, let me say to you that I also will not go down that road."

"Fair enough," he said, as if he were a Judge deciding that the case was closed. I could almost see him slamming down his gavel. He continued. "It seems that you're doing rather well for yourself, even won a few major awards. You know, I've heard you sing several times. I believe the name of the place was called The Jazz Cat."

"I doubt someone like you has ever been to a place like The Jazz Cat."

"I go to almost every business I own."

It were as if he'd just pulled a sign out of his pocket that said, "Gotcha!" And there was picture of me plastered right on the front.

"Real estate and jazz clubs, how nice." It was sarcastic, but who cared.

"I was informed that you needed a place to work."

Now, instead of a sign, I saw the biggest, brightest yellow billboard posted on the busiest street corner there was. He was making it harder for me not to show that he had me. You know that saying "Whoever looks away first, loses?" Well, I had to break the mind-wrecking eye contact we had going on and just look at my desk for a second. It was the only thing I could think of to do to try to get some of my color back.

I was about to slide off some response that I knew I wouldn't be proud of, when she walked in. You could tell just by the expression on her face that she was a box full of nasty colors.

She sat down next to her husband dusting off the seat first. Her ivory suit was pressed as new and crisp as if she had just worn it out of the store. She wore very little makeup, she didn't need any. Her fingers were long and slender, just like the rest of her, and yet I was sure she'd had never seen the inside of a gym.

I quickly calculated my roots. I knew that the beast had married at a young age, eighteen I believe. He'd been married only two years when his wife was killed in a car accident; they were just able to deliver my mother before she died. My mother gave birth to me at fifteen. She died right afterward. So these people in front of me now, the ones who started these roots, had to be around seventy, give or take a year or so. And yet still they made a classic picture of beauty and money.

"Shall I call you grandmother or great-grandmother?" I said to her.

"I have always been rather fond of my name," she said. "So why don't we start there."

"Do you know what Jonathan did with my son?" I asked her.

She looked at me like I had said a dirty word. "Jonathan? You mean your father?"

"No, I mean your son." The tension in our mutual glare was unmistakable, and I wanted to cross the table and put a wrinkle in that ivory suit.

But before either of them could respond, my secretary walked in and set some documents on my desk.

"What are these?" I asked. She didn't respond. I thought I was going to have to ask again when Kenneth reminded me that not only was he present, but wanted to be the one in charge.

"I asked her to bring in the documents required for your signature," he said. "So that we could finalize our business here today."

"I didn't agree to sell you my husband's property."

"Sure you will. Why would you want to keep a place he took other women to while he left you sitting at home in an apartment no bigger than this office?"

Then it was her turn. "Naya, I'm sure you will find our offer for the property beyond fair."

"It's Jazzmyne."

"I don't do stage names, dear. You were born with the name Naya and, therefore, I shall call you that."

All over again, I felt like the young, dumb little girl planting my feet on the ground of New York for the first time. I was allowing them to color me, and both of them knew it. I had to get control, had to not just dig deep but dive to the bottom of the well and scoop up whatever courage was left, so that I could allow my words to exhale.

I picked up the phone and called my secretary into the room. When she came in, I took a deep, long breath. And when I released it, it sounded a little something like this. "Connie, take these documents and be sure to hand them to Mr. and Mrs. Creek on their way out. This property has already been sold."

"I thought you indicated that you had not made a decision to sell," the ivory suit said, now a little flushed in the face.

I put that mind-wrecking eye contact back in place, looking at her with pure focus. "I believe what I said was that I had not agreed to sell *you* my husband's property. Like you said, why would I want to keep it? This morning, however, I agreed to sell the property to another buyer whose offer was also beyond fair."

Getting your color back was indeed a beautiful thing.

○ ◉ ○

# Chapter 22

"My anger and anxiety that day were enough to give me nightmares the rest of my life."

○◉○

# Nightmares

I watched both of them walk out of my office and stroll down the corridor as if it were all in a day's business. It didn't seem to matter who I was, especially not to her.

My anger and anxiety that day were enough to give me nightmares the rest of my life. I tried to leave hatred out of my thoughts, but even today, that is a battle I haven't won. That night, the burning still haunted me, making me break out in sweats, causing me to lose my mind. Lack of peace continued to be my real-life nightmare. It toyed with me, played with my emotions.

Although I admit there were days when I felt I had put out the flame for good, that picture of me and my son always crept back into the cracks of my denial. So I found myself picking up the phone and dialing those all-too-familiar digits that always brought more than a smile to my heart.

"That rough, huh?" he said. It often amazed me how well he knew my emotions, even through a telephone.

"Yes, but I managed to save my color."

"Did you get anything?"

"Not one syllable in response to my question about my son. But I swear, Chris, they know something."

"We tried," he said. "I warned you about them. I knew it would be a long shot, but I thought you needed to meet them one way or another. They make up parts of who you are, whether you'd like to admit that or not."

"If I never saw them again, it would be too soon."

"You will see them again."

"Why is that?"

"I already invited them to our wedding. I had to. I work for their firm and you are their great-granddaughter, give or take."

"Chris . . ."

"It's time Jazzmyne, to allow the Naya in you to come out. You don't have to worry, she's all grown up. It's time to end the nightmares." He then paused but only for a moment, "Marry me Naya."

"That would mean you'd have to quit."

"I will take that as a yes."

"You know me well enough that I don't need to answer."

"You're right. I do," he said. "But if you don't mind…" I didn't let him finish, I quickly gave my response.

"Chris," I said, almost in a faint whisper. "I will marry you."

"Naya?"

"Yes, Chris?"

"I already love the sound of Naya Moná Wesley, and I love you."

"I know you do."

"Since the beginning." he said, just before placing the receiver on the hook.

So on the eve of my third album release, Chris and I stood before each other and gave each other something precious: honesty—and all that came along with that. The album, *Jazzmyne's Happiness*, made record history.

In the three years that followed, the memory of our wedding day, buying a home together, and all the days that followed kept me happy enough to be in denial about wanting to meet my son. But after that point, as much as I tried to rid myself of those flames, I couldn't. The burning not only returned; this time it had decided to move in for good.

I knew he had to be around thirteen years old by then, so we hired private detective after private detective to try to find him, but every single one of them took my money and delivered me nothing but false hope. I had just about given up.

Then late one evening, I had come home after a hard, long day in the recording studio. I had just created the record label: *Jazzmyne's Lyrics*—which had about six other artists signed to it, and since Chris had started his own practice by then, our time together had gotten rather tight. So when I walked in the door and saw Chris sitting in the foyer, I knew that something was amiss; he never made it home before me.

"What happened?" I said.

"Kenneth and Sarah were killed in a car accident."

I wondered if the beast knew. But the only way for me to find out was to go back to the place I once called home.

# Chapter 23

"Now here I was on the road to home, arriving not theway
(formatting)
I left. Yet, I could still feel the darkness calling out to me as
it had so many years before. I wondered if my memories of
home would always leave the little girl in me, groping for
freedom in the darkness. I knew that if I could never forget
my past, then how could I ever truly be free?" (formatting)

◯ ◉ ◯

# The Road to Home

Once upon a time, I left my father's home. A thousand dollars in my pocket, blood on my clothes and the burning desire to find freedom in my heart. Now here I was on the road to home, arriving not the way I left. Yet, I could still feel the darkness calling out to me as it had so many years before. I wondered, if my memories of home would always leave the little girl in me, groping for freedom in the darkness. I knew that if I could never forget my past, then how could I ever truly be free? No amount of money can erase my past, unless I faced it and moved on, it will always be in my crayon box.

When the car pulled up to the apartment building, all I could do was sit. Chris squeezed my hand, but my heart, my mind, and my colors were still throbbing with the anxiety of the moment. All I had to do was go inside those doors, up one flight of stairs, and around a right corner and I would be standing outside the door of pain.

It was a hard potential reality to embrace. So hard it took me a solid fifteen minutes just to attempt to reach out and grab hold of it. It took me another fifteen minutes or so to walk up the steps and just a few more to make that right turn, but, finally, I stood at a point where nothing separated the beast and I but a door. Chris had to knock for me.

We waited for what seemed like an eternity, but was simply seconds of time that added up to a very long moment. Someone came to the door, only it wasn't him. It was a young woman, probably around thirteen, with butterscotch skin and hazel brown eyes. She told us that he had left the day before on a flight to New York to attend his parent's funeral.

I was relieved, but I decided that the only way to go was to face the beast at the funeral. The flight back to New

York was brought with it mixed emotions and a comment from Chris that didn't surprise me much.

"She looked like a slightly younger version of you," he said. I agreed but could say nothing.

The day of the funeral rolled around like it had been waiting for me. I woke up determined to face the skeletons in my closet, as they say. I only wished that my body had agreed. But my body, it seems, had decided to come down with the worst case of food poisoning I'd ever had. The coincidence was strange but true. I couldn't even get out of bed without throwing up all over the place. And though it was a rough reality to accept, I had no choice but to close that window to my past for the moment.

As soon as I was well enough, I flew back to Chicago, but only to find that the beast had moved out. I wished I had known then that he'd moved to New York.

The next ten years flew past me like it had a plane to catch. Chris and I had kept up a search that entire time, but still nothing. Then finally a break came.

Chris overheard some former coworkers at the local attorney hangout saying how sad it was that the Creek Real Estate Group was in trouble. They said that ever since the

Creek's son had taken over, the company had suffered so many severe losses that many were scared the doors would soon be closed.

It didn't take us long to get our private detectives to start earning all the money we'd dished out to them over the years. But when one of them came back one day and told us that the beast was living in New York in his parent's home, I couldn't believe my ears. Tears began to stream down my face almost instantly.

Chris and I wasted no time, later that week; we drove up to the Creeks' once-upon-a-time residence. I didn't even care about reliving the past. I didn't care what the beast had done to me, and I didn't care how much I hated him. All I cared about was asking the question "Where is my son?" It turned out that he knew we were coming and was ready to provide an answer.

As soon as our car pulled up to the protective gate, it began to open, and we drove past the trees and down a driveway. I didn't look at anything else; I was waiting for that front door to come into my view. As soon as it did, I jumped out and ran up the never-ending flight of steps like I was simply walking on clouds. I could hear Chris behind me. Both our hearts were pounding so loudly with the sound not knowing what lay just ahead.

When I finally managed to ring the bell, reality answered the door in the form of an old man. He tried to put on a smile, but I could tell he wasn't happy with the message he had to deliver us, which was tucked tightly between his fingers in a yellow envelope marked "To my daughter." He handed it to me quickly and then tried very politely to excuse himself, sliding back behind the large wood door and closing it quickly. I didn't care about that either.

As Chris and I walked down the stairs, I was holding that yellow envelope in my hands, when something told me to turn around and look up. Standing in the window on the second floor, watching me, was the beast. Chris saw him too, but neither of us cared much about that either— at least not enough in that moment to stop and go back. What was there to say, the beast had aged. Enough said.

**⊙**

# Chapter 24

"I knew that this was the moment I would find out about you—and I didn't want the beast to be in it."

## ◯ ⊙ ◯

# This Is the Moment

I was back in the moment of the present again, watching the emotions on my son's face while trying to maintain my own.

I knew he was asking himself, "Why didn't I just open the envelope right then and there, right on the front steps of the Creek mansion?" So, I decided to take the initiative and provide the answer.

"Let me tell you," I explained, "that envelope felt like it was ready to explode in my hands. I was so eager to find out what it said. But then I knew that this was the moment I would find out about you—and I didn't want that beast to be in it."

"So I waited until we were finally back at our home, in our own moment, in our own living room—sitting on our sofa; each of us, staring at the envelope, but neither of us saying a word. I can't begin to explain to you what it was like when I finally opened it. The emotions, that boiled up and spilled over into my husband's hands as he held me. But in that envelope was a picture of you. And then there was this letter."

I handed him the white lined paper with J. K.'s blue-inked handwriting. He immediately took it. This is what he read:

*To my daughter Naya,*

*Over the years, I have wanted to mail some version of this letter to you. I think once I made it to the mail box, pulled down the box opening, looked inside and tried to imagine my letter in there with all the rest. I find myself every year doing a rewrite. I'm not going to write a letter of apologizes although that would be appropriate. It's just that I honestly don't think that my saying I'm sorry would help the matter much. But for the record, I am very much so.*

*You can't inhale the reality of what drove me to my madness; it would be too much for you. Only now, as an older man, can I even begin to comprehend it. Ten years ago my Father decided to pick up the telephone only to tell me that he had visited you and that you had wanted to know about Jonathan. I admit I still wasn't in my right mind at that point, but, I think it was that moment that made me begin to turn the corner and face the nightmare that I had created for myself.*

*There is a history behind me, no— inside me, that I can't even try to relate to you. Although I know that I should try. Maybe my hesitation is that I still believe you wouldn't understand. Perhaps, the truth of the matter is that I fear that you wouldn't really care. Why should you?*

*Hatred can cover up everything if you let it, even the truth. Hatred has a way of creeping into the depths of your corners and staying there. It has a way of sinking into your veins and coming out through your pores. In the end, hatred can make you become a beast. Please let the hatred for me move from the thing that drives it, your heart. Only then can you get back all that I took from you.*

*I'm going to wrap this letter up and make it brief because I don't think you really care about the rest, although one day I hope to explain it to you face-to-face. In fact, I need to explain it to you face-to-face. I owe myself that.*

*I know you're probably thinking what a thing to say…as if I owe myself anything, but I do. I owe myself a sense of peace even if it is just a sense. I owe you the full version, can't skimp on that even if my thoughts begged me to. One day.*

*I think I feel something as I write this that I have never felt before, a tear drop. Can a father cry for one that never should have been his?*

*Getting to the reason for my letter…..*

*I gave Jonathan to my parents when he was born. I know it's no secret that my madness couldn't bear the thought of having a son. You see it wasn't something even she wanted...sorry about that statement. I find myself caught between the present and the O' so long ago memories that are constantly floating inside my head.*

*Jonathan was raised by her; I mean "them", until they were killed in a car accident as you are already aware. How I miss him, my father, that is. I did what I could for Jonathan for another five years. That doesn't count for much, probably nothing at all really, but it was the only way I could even attempt to do something right in my life.*

*It seems in the end, all we really want is to have something we do right, count. Isn't that a funny thing? In fact, I don't think I pondered much over that very fact until now.*

*I'm sorry... I'm getting back to the information you want.*

*At the point of my writing you this, Jonathan should be finishing up Grad school. He is very smart, hand-*

*some (I know that didn't come from me) and very strong-minded. When he left here at eighteen, I knew that he would never be back. And so I haven't spoken to him since, but, I have tried to keep up with his whereabouts as much as possible.*

*I have enclosed the only photograph I had of him that I got out of my parent's photo album; I think he's around ten in it. I also included the address I had for him at the school he is attending. I'm not sure if he's really ready to handle the truth about matters but I'll leave that up to you to decide. Tell me are you ready for that moment?*

*J.K.*

*P.S. If I could ever go back to the days of just being your father, I would like that very much, but if not, know that I understand. It was great to see you sing.*

The moment of silence had crept into the air again. I was sitting on the sofa, watching my son with the letter still in the tight grip of his hands. His eyes still gazing over the sentences; I waited.

When he was finished reading, he looked up at me. "I don't understand. If you knew where I was at this point, why didn't you try to contact me then? Why did you wait another ten-plus years to pick up the phone and call me."

"Because I realized he was right. You weren't ready to hear how once-upon-a-time I looked into what I thought were the eyes of my father's son. Too be honest, I discovered then that I wasn't even ready for that moment.

"How does one pick a moment in their life, to say the words that have been a part of their thoughts, conversation, emotions, and even journey for what seemed an eternity?"

"So what changed?"

"I don't know exactly, but I woke up one day, turned to my husband and said 'this is the moment' and he agreed."

"So where is he now?"

"The beast? Oh, he passed away two years ago."

"I knew that, I meant your husband, where is he?"

"He thought that we needed this week to ourselves, so he's staying at one of our other properties."

"So you got into real estate?"

"Real estate and jazz clubs, I told you the color of Jazzmyne runs deep."

Moving off that subject I asked, "So where do you want to go from here?" I took a deep breath, trying to suck all the anticipation of the response in.

"You know when I first came here, all I could think about, was telling you that no matter what you said, no matter what story you told, it would never remove the anger that dwelled in my heart. It would never replace the anger that lived in my thoughts and kept me up most of my life. But now, none of that seems to matter to me anymore. I realize that for me, this is the moment that I've dreamt about, it's time for my family to meet my roots."

To say, that my heart began to beat heavily at that possibility would be an understatement. To say, that my mind created so many thoughts about the emotions that I would feel, the colors that would now be in my box, with each hug would be putting things mildly. But know, that when I looked into the eyes of my grandchildren and held the hand of my son's wife, I felt like Naya Moná was finally back.

I now understood one vital fact, one full second of intense and pure wisdom. I had to embrace my past. I had to allow my colors to form on their own. And that it's okay to create new colors in my box. I finally understood how to color me Jazzmyne.

However, having said all that, I now understood why my son wanted to know my roots. I still needed to know about my father's roots. There were too many unanswered questions that I had from the letter. I need to go back into his history. That flame was still flickering in my mind, wavering in my heart and causing my sense of freedom to be questioned.

How I wondered about Jonathan's colors; the beast that is. One day, that box will be opened.

For now, Jonathan and I appeared to be making our way back to the possibility of reality. No longer would I be a once-upon-a-time mother. I am Naya Moná, the Jazz singer, the wife, the mother. This is who I was meant to be.

The conversation had drifted off and we both stood up in an effort to allow the moment to sink into our thoughts. Smiles were upon our faces. I began to walk toward the phone to call Chris and welcome him home. I saw Jonathan walk over toward my window and pull back the sheer panel. He then turned toward me and asked.... "Did you ever find out who the young girl was that came to the door that day you went to Chicago to visit your father?"

I held the phone receiver in my hand and when I looked up at him I felt the corners of my eyes twitch upward and a slow grin spread across my face. How deep my colors go.

**The End...Of course not!**

# About the Author

I admit that I hesitate to write this section, it's hard believe it or not, to write about oneself. However, it seems that the question that everyone seems to ask me—when I even hinted at the fact that I was working on this project, is, "did you include an 'About the Author' section in your book?" To which, my response was more than often—a firm no, until now.

Here it is 5:12 on a Saturday morning and I find myself giving in to the pressure. Don't we all at some point in our life? I also find myself contemplating the question... What would people want to know about me? The other day (speaking of course the day or so before I sat down to write this) I was speaking to a close friend of mine and of course we were discussing this book. It has been the topic of conversation for a couple of weeks, as she often listened to me ramble on, trying to get my thoughts together.

She started asking me questions so much so, that I thought that I was on a radio station being interviewed. It was okay, she was right in the fact that the questions that she posed are ones that some who read the book, might want to know. Maybe not some, but hopefully a few million—every writers dream it seems. So I've decided to do something different and present this like the website bio, question and answer.

If you've been to the site at www.lbpublishing.com then you probably know that I was born in Chicago, Illinois. I lived about eight or nine years of my later years in Oak Park, Illinois where I attended High School. It was a school the size of a college.

I moved in the summer after my junior year to Atlanta, GA where I finished up the rest of my High School and College years. I'm sure by now, you've heard enough about where I come from.

**Question: Have you always wanted to write?**

"Yes and no. I always enjoyed writing but I don't think I took it seriously until my second year in high school when I originally thought about this book. In fact, I wrote a different version of it. You see, the story has been in my head lurking around it seems since then."

**Question: How long did it take you to write this book?**

"That is a tough question because if you count the original version, then it took almost 20+ years. I would write a page or two and then walk away from it. Get started in some other color in my life and then I would remember this story. Now that I've used that word 'color' to describe a time in my life, you are probably thinking about the next question."

**Question: Is Jazzmyne about you?**

"I tried to tackle this one on the site because it is the first thing I am asked, as soon as I begin to describe what happens to the main character that contributes to all the colors in her life. While the character is not a reflection of myself, she does represent some of the emotions and attitudes that I honestly feel we all have had or experienced throughout our journey in life. We all have many colors in our crayon box."

**Question: What is the concept of the book based on?**

"When writing this book I tried to envision each character on a screen and then as I placed my fingers upon the keypad of my laptop, I tried to capture all that I saw as I typed. Is it a touchy-feely type of book? Yes, in many ways it is. Does it have drama? Of course, don't we all? Is there romance? I'm a woman, so yes; there is romance but just a little. "

**Question: Are you going to write another book?**

"Yes. I want to write another one, although I admit that this one kept me up a many nights. However, I feel that when you take on something like this, it often will— kept you up late at night. Maybe one day, I will get to the point when writing a book doesn't. I am sure that will be a long time coming. Positive, actually."

**Question: Will it be a continuation of this book?**

"It will be based off a character in this book but not necessarily a continuation of this one."

**Question: Do you have a name for the new book?**

"It will be called: 'My Father's Colors.'

**In conclusion:**

To everyone who has supported me I just want to say thank you. Some, I know will love the book, some won't. Some will be somewhere in between. How each of us views things in our life, often depends upon the colors in our box.

*Marian L. Thomas*